"You are beautiful beyond all other women, Jessie," said Henri. "You are more than beautiful. You are a mystery."

"What mystery do you see in me, Henri?" she murmured.

"Ah, my Jessie—"

Suddenly they heard a noise, heavy-footed over the floor upstairs. Then they saw him—his features were twisted with rage. He held a torch in his left hand and a dynamite bomb in his right.

"Stay where you are, Baron!" Jessie yelled.

Baron Heligendorf touched the fuse of the dynamite to the flame...

→ WESLEY ELLIS ←

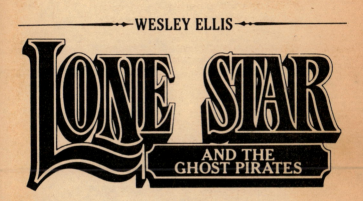

LONE STAR

AND THE GHOST PIRATES

A JOVE BOOK

LONE STAR AND THE GHOST PIRATES

A Jove Book / published by arrangement with
the author

PRINTING HISTORY
Jove edition / January 1984

ISBN: 0-515-07396-2

PRINTED IN THE UNITED STATES OF AMERICA

LONE STAR
AND
THE GHOST PIRATES

★

Chapter 1

Jebediah Adams had not been to sea for twenty years, but he still affected the brass-buttoned blue coat of the sailing captain he had once been. His gray whiskers were full, framing a solid, ruddy face, and his narrow blue eyes were sharp, as though he were squinting into a wind, searching a vacant sea for sight of land. He whipped his oak wheelchair impatiently around the corner of his huge desk and smiled, nodding, as he came rolling across the room toward Jessica Starbuck.

"Miss Starbuck, it is a genuine pleasure," he boomed heartily. "The pleasure could be greater only if—well, only if you had been brought here by your father, God rest him." He reached for her hand. "You look like him. You look like your mother. By the Eternal!"

Jessie let Captain Adams squeeze her hand in his great, callused palm. In an instant she liked the man. She glanced at Ki and saw that he liked the captain too. Instinctively they dispelled a suspicion they had mulled over all the way from Texas—that maybe Captain Adams, the general man-

1

ager, was himself the source of the problem with Starbuck Shipping.

"My father spoke of you often, Captain Adams," she said.

The captain nodded. He looked at Ki, "And you are Ki?"

Ki nodded.

Captain Adams looked up into Ki's placid, self-confident face, noting and conspicuously judging the Oriental cast of Ki's eyes, the sallow hue of his skin, his straight black hair. "Alex Starbuck told me about you," he said. "Any man who earned his confidence has mine."

"That is a compliment indeed," said Ki.

"Well," said the captain. Grasping the wheels, he rolled his chair back a pace. "Won't you sit down? I'll have coffee brought in. Or whiskey, if you prefer."

"I'd enjoy a cup of good coffee," said Jessica.

The captain kept a cane at hand, pushed down between his body and the arm of his wheelchair, and he reached out to the wall with it and gave a brass ship's bell that hung there a hard whack. A man's face appeared instantly in the door of the office, and the captain ordered coffee.

"If ever a man deserved success and wealth," said Captain Adams as he wheeled himself behind his desk, "it was your father, Miss Starbuck. I was with him in the Japans, you know. He was shrewd and brave. His assassination came as a great shock."

Jessica nodded. "To us all," she said.

"And now, I suppose, the sharks are about, trying to steal your inheritance."

"We've had some problems," said Jessica. "Cattle rustling. Land swindles. We've wondered, of course, if the troubles with our ships are part of the pattern."

The captain slapped the arm of his chair. "If I could get on my feet, I'd know," he growled. "Miss Starbuck, I'm sorry to have this news for you on your arrival here in New Orleans, but still another ship is missing. The *Abraham*. It was one of the first ships your father owned."

"Pirates," said Ki. "In the nineteenth century..."

"Well, they're not going down in storms," said the captain. "We have to think it's piracy on the high seas."

"All the missing ships are Starbuck ships," said Jessie.

"All four," said the captain.

"It's not just chance piracy, then," she said. "Obviously it's another part of this continuing war against anything bearing the Starbuck name."

"The people who killed your father..." said the captain quietly.

"The men who fired the guns that killed my father are dead, Captain Adams," Jessie said grimly. "And the men who hired them. But behind them..." She shook her head. "My father was at war, in a real sense. My mother was murdered. So was my father. The men who are ultimately responsible have tried to kill me, more than once."

"Being a woman—"

"Being a woman is a great advantage," said Jessie. "It makes them think what they want to do will be easy. But my father taught me to defend myself and to fight back. And—"

"And he gave you Ki," said the captain.

"Not 'gave' me," said Jessica. "Ki is not property. What's more, he is not my employee. He is my friend."

"I understand," said Captain Adams. "Don't forget, I was in the Japans, in my time. Your father explained to me who Ki is. Ki is a samurai."

"Yes," said Jessie. "He has pledged himself to me, to give me his friendship and his protection, all our lives. It is a relationship of honor. Mutual honor."

"I understand," said the captain.

"He will accompany me."

"Accompany you where, Miss Starbuck?"

"To sea, aboard the first Starbuck ship heading south. We will visit our office in Veracruz. We'll sail on from there. I mean to see for myself what's going on."

"Miss Starbuck," the captain said, "I can't be responsible—"

"No, and you won't be," said Jessie firmly.

The captain smiled. "Your father would have gone."

"And so will I."

Captain Adams filled his lungs with a deep, thoughtful breath. He nodded. "The *Sarah* sails on Friday. A packet, a thousand-tonner. She's named for your sainted mother. Your father was proud of the *Sarah*. She's one of the few ships he took a personal interest in, in his later years. She'll be calling at Veracruz."

"The *Sarah,* then," said Jessica.

"I'll see to it you're well put up, Miss Starbuck. All I wish is that I could come with you."

"I wish you could too, Captain Adams," said Jessie.

The corners of the old man's mouth turned down, and he shrugged. "My days at sea are over," he muttered. "You will, though, attend our ball tomorrow night? You won't deprive me of that pleasure, will you?"

"No, of course not, Captain," said Jessie. "We're looking forward to it. I've never been to a real New Orleans Mardi Gras."

"How fortunate that you should be in the city!" the captain said. "I have taken the liberty of having costumes made for each of you. I hope you will enjoy attending as Queen Elizabeth—and you, Ki, as Sir Walter Raleigh. It will be glorious!"

From her bedroom window in the captain's fine antebellum mansion, Jessie had a view of the Mississippi waterfront, of ranks of sternwheelers lined up at the wharves, of scores of seagoing vessels crowded together, their bowsprits extending over the levee. She had seen Europe and some of the Orient and most of the cities of North America, but she stood and stared with pleasure at the exotic scene laid out before her by New Orleans. Since her father's death, she had spent almost all her time at home on the ranch or traveling with Ki on urgent journeys to rough frontier towns where they fought the battles that were necessary to preserve what her father had built. Only last month she and Ki had been in the Badlands of the Dakota Territory—a rugged, chilly, dangerous place if ever she had seen one—where they had frustrated a land-stealing scheme directed against

4

the struggling farmers and ranchers of the area. Now, as she stood in this exquisitely furnished, comfortable room, she found it hard to believe that New Orleans and the Badlands could both be parts of the same nation, so vastly different were they from each other. It was tempting to entertain the notion that soft luxury such as this should be her birthright as the heiress of the Starbuck enterprises and the almost inconceivable fortune that went with them. She knew, though, that if she surrendered to that idea, she would risk not just the loss of her inheritance, but of her life as well. Her father's enemies did not want only to impoverish her, they wanted to kill her. She turned away from the window. She would enjoy Mardi Gras in New Orleans, but on Friday she would go aboard the *Sarah*, bound for southern Mexico and probably another encounter with the conspiracy that had killed her father and mother.

The captain's upstairs maid, a strange, dark Cajun woman, had adjusted her Queen Elizabeth costume to fit her. It was a handsome silk dress of shimmering green that set off the copper highlights in her honey-blond hair, and it was extremely unlikely that any Queen of England had ever worn anything like it. As a concession to the occasion, Jessie had allowed herself to be loaded with an excess of glass gems and a fancy starched collar meant to suggest a sixteenth-century ruff. She had, however—now that the Cajun maid was gone—removed the collar and also the lace panel intended to cover and hide her decolletage. The dress was cut low, but she guessed it would not scandalize the celebrants of Fat Tuesday. She had been given a brief introduction to the traditions of Mardi Gras since yesterday, and she was not reluctant to hide her face behind her mask and uncover her breasts to the edges of her aureoles. It would be modest, she had been told, compared to some of the costumes she would see tonight.

Once the maid was gone, Jessie had hoisted her skirts around her hips and affixed to her leg the garter holster that carried her derringer. She was hardly ever without the derringer. When she dropped the skirt, the little pistol was safely hidden in a most private place.

"Come in," she said a moment later, in response to a knock on the door.

Ki came in, shaking his head. He did look ludicrous as a Japanese Walter Raleigh—in red velvet and silk hose, a floppy red velvet hat, and shoes with turned-up toes. She had to laugh. "You'll be masked," she said, grinning. "That's the salvation of your dignity."

He appraised the cut of her dress. "What saves yours?" he asked. "Everyone will know who you are."

"And I'm going to enjoy it immensely," she said.

They rode to the Andrew Jackson Hotel in the captain's gleaming black carriage. The captain was costumed as a Chinese mandarin, in a voluminous yellow silk robe, and he was attended by a manservant dressed as a coolie, who would push his wheelchair.

The streets were alive with revelers, and the carriage made its way with difficulty through a noisy, drunken, happy throng. Jessica saw that the crowd troubled Ki. Then she saw something that only she could detect and understand. Ki seemed to withdraw within himself as he began a controlled, rhythmic breathing. It was how he calmed himself and concentrated his energy. If there were actually danger in the crowd around their carriage, Ki would know it first and would react first. He had trained his senses, and beyond that, he seemed to have special instincts that were not of the senses.

"I've loved Mardi Gras ever since I came to settle in New Orleans," said Captain Adams. "Ever since Alex Starbuck asked me to manage his shipping interests."

"I could learn to love it," said Jessie, peering out the window of the carriage at a line of grotesquely masked dancers bobbing along the street.

Only Ki knew they were being attacked. As Jessie and the captain talked, Ki noticed two men moving purposefully in the crowd. The nature of their movements was enough to alert him. They moved faster than the others, more abruptly, shouldering their way among the revelers. The broad grins on their masks were inconsistent with the urgency of their progress toward the carriage. He watched them from the corners of his eyes, never turning his head directly toward them, until one of them threw himself suddenly toward the carriage door, raising a sawed-off shotgun from under his oversized costume coat. Ki had been sitting quietly with his right hand inside his Elizabethan doublet. Now, in a motion so quick, short, and apparently relaxed that even Jessie didn't notice it, he withdrew the hand, flicking it in the same movement toward the approaching gunman. Nor did Jessie see how the man in the grinning mask clutched at his throat and, in the last moment of his life, instinctively tried to pull out the star-shaped, razorlike disk that had embedded itself in his trachea. The carriage moved on before the man slumped to the pavement, falling on his shotgun. His companion knelt over the fallen man. He looked up, and for an instant his gaze met Ki's. Ki could see his eyes, glittering ominously from behind his mask. That man would remember Ki always, but Ki had not really seen his face and would not know him when he saw him again.

The grand ballroom of the Andrew Jackson Hotel was lighted by a thousand gas jets and candles that threw a flattering golden light on three hundred costumed ladies and gentlemen who dined and drank and danced under the benign and placid watch of a masked man and woman who reigned from a dais as king and queen of the ball. A string orchestra played beneath the dais. Servants, also masked, attended the guests, keeping their plates and glasses filled. A happy clamor of talk rose above the calm music of the violins. The excitement of the street was absent here. These revelers were more comfortable than excited.

Still, they were revelers. She had never seen people costumed in public the way these prosperous ladies and gentlemen of New Orleans dressed for Fat Tuesday. As she had been led to expect, her decolletage won her appreciative glances but no shocked stares. Ladies dressed as women from the French court were showing even their nipples, and

7

had reddened them with rouge, too. More astonishing, a group of young women dressed as Egyptian harem girls passed by on their way to their table, barefoot and showing their legs through sheer pantaloons. Jessie was surprised and amused.

At Captain Adams's table there was only one woman besides Jessie. She, Mrs. Galbraith, was the wife of Jefferson Galbraith, introduced by the captain as a leading cotton factor and a heavy user of Starbuck shipping services. A corpulent, late-middle-aged woman, Mrs. Galbraith had come dressed as a covered-up plantation belle and was unable to conceal her disapproval of Jessica's low-cut dress — or her disapproval of the conspicuous approval it gained from the six men at the table.

Sitting opposite Jessie was Jonathan Brentwood, a foppish young man in satin and powdered wig who complained petulantly that he had been seated too far from "Miz Stahbook." He was from Vicksburg and represented his father, who sent barrels of whiskey down the Mississippi for shipment via Starbuck vessels to Galveston, whence the product was shipped by train and wagon to saloons all across Texas.

At Jessie's left was a Frenchman, Henri Derval, who was in America temporarily, representing his family's business—the exporting of wines from France. He was a handsome, blue-eyed man with a strong chin, who spoke with an accent that Jessie found charming. His costume for the night was the uniform of a Napoleonic general, complete with epaulettes and sword.

"I am overjoyed," he said, "to learn that I am to have the good fortune to sail on Friday for Veracruz on the same ship with you, Miss Starbuck."

"Oh, you're traveling on the *Sarah?*"

Henri Derval nodded. "I understand it was named for your mother."

"Yes."

"It must please your mother very much to have so handsome a ship named for her."

"She never knew about it. My father bought it and named it for her only after her death."

"She must have died young, then."

"She was murdered."

"Mon Dieu!" the Frenchman gasped.

"As was my father."

"My regrets, Mam'selle. I am sorry to have recalled to your mind such tragic events on so beautiful a night."

"It's all right. You may call me Jessie. If we are going to be sailing all the way to Veracruz on the same small ship, we are going to become well acquainted."

Henri Derval smiled. "I most certainly hope so—Jessie."

Seated next to Ki was a beefy German who said his name was Otto vom und zum Heligendorf—*Baron* Otto vom und zum Heligendorf. He was introduced by Captain Adams as another shipper on Starbuck ships. He represented a German company that bought and sold arms and ammunition, exporting some from Europe to America, but also buying some items in America for shipment to Europe. He had, the captain said, bought surplus Union Army field guns in great numbers after the late War of the Rebellion and sold them in various countries in Central and South America. He, too, would be aboard the *Sarah* on her voyage to Mexico, accompanying his cargo, which would be in the hold—a thousand French "needle guns" he had brokered to the government of Mexico. The baron was costumed as a courtier at the court of Louis XV, in pink satin and a powdered wig. Ki detected that he was unhappy to be seated beside an Oriental who—however he was introduced—was probably a servant to the young lady across the table.

"You are—Chinese?" he asked loftily.

"No," said Ki. "Japanese. Half Japanese, actually. My mother was Japanese. My father was American."

"A sailor?"

"A businessman," said Ki coldly, disliking the implication. "My mother's family are titled."

He did not add that his mother's family had disowned her for marrying a "barbarian" and had never recognized him. Nor did he explain that his parents' death left him an impoverished urchin, an unwelcome half-breed. He was a samurai because he had been trained to it through apprenticeship to a demanding old warrior.

"I have never been to Japan," said the baron, dismissing Ki with that comment and turning his conversational attention to the Galbraiths.

Jessie danced with Henri Derval. He was tall; his arms were strong. He had, he said, fought as an officer in the army of Louis Napoleon in the brief war of 1870. He had been at Sedan and personally witnessed his country's disastrous defeat at the hands of the invading Germans. Baron vom und zum Heligendorf had been there too, he said—as a Prussian officer.

"You know the baron, then?" she asked.

"Unfortunately, yes."

Jessica laughed. "You don't like him."

"I detest him. I am thrown in his company often, since we travel in business, and the world of international businessmen is not so very large after all. He never omits an occasion for reminding me of how his army defeated mine in 1870."

"Henri . . ." Jessica murmured.

"Jessie?"

"Why don't you forget the baron for tonight and concentrate on the woman in your arms?"

★

Chapter 2

The *Sarah* was a 170-foot packet of one thousand tons,
three-masted, copper-sheathed below the waterline, rugged,
entirely capable of long voyages across the Atlantic or Pa-
cific—but, in the 1880s, hard put to compete with the great
windjammers and steam-powered ships that now dominated
the long-distance trade. The *Sarah* remained a proud ship,
but in this decade she was more suited to the coastal trade
she plied—New Orleans to Galveston to Tampico to Veracruz to Havana to Kingston to Port-au-Prince, sometimes
to Caracas, and home again to New Orleans—than to the
long ocean crossings that the bigger clippers and steam-
powered ships could sail faster.

The *Sarah* could carry twenty-five cabin-class passengers. In her first decade she had carried Europeans to America in steerage—thousands of them over the years—but
since she had been bought by Alex Starbuck and renamed,
she had carried cargo in her gloomy holds and no passengers
she could not accommodate in cabins. In the style of her
time, she was painted black above the waterline, with a
broad white stripe running along her side. Black squares

painted on her stripe were intended to suggest gunports, but few potential pirates would have failed to understand that the *Sarah* carried no guns that amounted to anything. She was equipped with water closets and with big iron tanks for drinking water. She had a good reputation as a comfortable, modern coastal transport—which was why, probably, she carried such passengers on this voyage as Henri Derval and the Baron Otto vom und zum Heligendorf.

The crew knew the owner was aboard. The captain had vacated his cabin at the stern, and Jessica's trunk had been installed there. Extra attention had been given to holystoning the decks, and weatherbeaten surfaces had been touched up with paint. Crewmen had put aside ragged sea clothing and waited on deck in their most respectable whites. The captain himself, in blues with brass buttons, waited on the poop.

All of them were surprised at the young woman who alighted from a carriage on the quay and strode purposefully up the gangplank. Most of the sailors and officers had never before seen a woman in pants, much less in worn and faded skintight blue jeans, wearing a revolver in a holster slung on her hip. She wore, too, a checkered shirt, boots, and a brown Stetson that hung on its chin thong behind her shoulders. The breeze caught and stirred her unbound long blond hair. She was anything but self-conscious. She nodded at the officer who greeted her at the top of the gangplank and turned immediately for the poop.

The captain of the *Sarah* was Cabell Baldwin. He was a rotund, ruddy, red-haired but balding man of fifty. As Jessie approached and mounted the ladder to the poopdeck, he tossed his cigar overboard and removed his cap and tucked it under his arm.

"Miss Starbuck," he said. "It is a distinct honor." He spoke with a slight lisp. "Welcome aboard."

She nodded and said it was good to be aboard. She was not offended by his open appraisal of her clothes and body. She was accustomed to that and could have dressed like Mrs. Galbraith at the ball if she were offended by male appreciation.

"We will cast off at dawn, if it suits you," said Captain Baldwin.

"As you judge, Captain," she said. "Handle the ship as your experience and knowledge suggest."

"Thank you, ma'am. I, uh, have placed you in my cabin for the voyage. Mr. Ki has the first officer's cabin, the next one."

"I'm sorry to inconvenience you, Captain."

"The passenger stateroom I've taken is quite comfortable, ma'am."

"Is Monsieur Derval on board?"

"He is, ma'am. Also Baron Heligendorf. We have eighteen passengers for the voyage. We are fortunate in having Monsieur Derval. He will supply fine wines for our table, as he always does."

"Seat him beside me, Captain," said Jessie. "And put the baron at the opposite end of the table."

Captain Baldwin smiled as he bowed. "As you wish, ma'am," he said.

Ki joined her in her cabin shortly after she was introduced to it. He glanced around and remarked that it was better suited to a sea captain than to her. The cabin was in fact roomy, though furnished with heavy, leather-upholstered furniture bolted to the deck. A wide window, not just a porthole, opened through the stern, affording her a view just now of the river, with rafts and scows busily moving up and down. Ki checked the lock on her door, frowned, and pronounced it inadequate.

"Do you want to sleep in here with me?" she asked, half playfully.

"I will sleep with my door open," he said.

Ki had told her about the man who tried to shove a shotgun through their carriage window on the way to the ball. The incident had convinced them, if they needed convincing, that the cartel was behind the loss of Starbuck ships. Why would pirates seek to kill the owner in New Orleans, before she had so much as set foot on a ship?

13

"I am uneasy about the ship," said Ki.

"Because we are, in a sense, imprisoned on it?" she asked.

"There is no retreat from it," he said gravely. "Once we are at sea, whatever faces us, we must cope with it in the narrow confines of these decks."

"The captain?" she asked.

He shrugged. "I cannot judge him yet. Do you judge your Frenchman is a friend?"

"Henri? I think so. As for the baron, it's too easy to suspect him. And there are sixteen others aboard."

"I will remain close to you," said Ki.

They had dinner in the saloon at seven, with only eight of the passengers as yet aboard. Jessie dressed for dinner in gray silk, and Henri introduced her to the wines he exported and was carrying in quantity in the hold—fine champagne chilled in ice, which he had brought aboard for this first dinner, and aged Bordeaux to accompany their roast beef. The ship provided the brandy that was poured with their coffee, but it too was a Derval import. After dinner, surfeited with food and a little giddy from the wine and brandy, Jessie went on deck with Henri, to take the air and look at the port in the yellow moonlight.

The dockside was clamorous. Draymen hurried to this ship and others, bringing the rest of the passengers for the *Sarah*, with their baggage, bringing some huge crates, final items of cargo to be lashed in the hold before the ship sailed. The town itself, beyond the quay, was alive. Lights burned everywhere, and distant music suggested the lively pleasures for which New Orleans was famous.

"A French city," Henri remarked. "The only one you have, unfortunately."

Jessie grinned at him. "Maybe one is enough," she said.

She turned and walked to the river side of the deck, where she could look out over the dark water which was alive even at night with boats and rafts. Henri followed her and stood beside her at the rail. He stood close. She felt his hip and shoulder lightly touching hers.

"You know why I am aboard this ship, I suppose," she said.

"You have lost four ships," he said. "I have lost two cargoes, worth a hundred thousand francs."

"Aren't you afraid you might lose the cargo you have aboard?" she asked.

"No," he said simply.

"No? Why not?"

Turning his eyes away from the river, he looked directly at her. "This ship is safe, I'm sure," he said. "It carries a score of passengers. Your other ships, the ones you lost, were not of this quality. They carried only three or four passengers, if any—because they did not offer the amenities offered by the *Sarah*. I don't think the pirates are willing to become kidnappers of prominent people."

"Still—"

"Jessie," he said, "if I lose a cargo of wines to Caribbean pirates, my government protests, but not very loudly. If, on the other hand, I, a French citizen, the son of a prominent family, am kidnapped by those pirates, my government might send gunboats into the Caribbean—or at least demand that your government do so. The same is true of Baron Heligendorf. His government—"

"Has the baron also lost cargoes?" she asked.

"Yes."

"Of weapons?"

"Yes."

"Still, he has a cargo in the hold." She frowned. "Why do you and the baron still put cargoes on Starbuck ships, if those are the only ones being taken by pirates?"

"Speaking for myself," said Henri, "it is because my family has been shipping wines and brandies on Starbuck ships for a decade, always with pleasure in the meticulous care given our cargoes by your company. We are not ready to abandon you so easily. As for the baron, I am not sure his motives are the same."

"Tell me more about the baron."

"I wish I knew more about him. He deals in arms, as you know—not strictly on his own account, but as the representative of a group of backers who wish to remain anonymous. There is little doubt that some of his transactions involve the corruption of governments. Your own government, for example, has sold him stocks of weapons left over from your Civil War."

"Where is the corruption in that?" Jessie asked.

"A few months ago," said Henri, "he sold one hundred artillery pieces, twelve pounders, to the government of Bolivia for two hundred dollars apiece. That is less than it cost your government to manufacture those guns. If he sold them for two hundred dollars each, we know he bought them for much less. Someone in your government sold him those cannon for less than half of what it cost to make them."

"A sharp trader," Jessica commented.

Henri nodded, fell silent, and stared out across the black river.

Ki had overheard the conversation. As he often did when they were in new surroundings, Ki had explored the ship thoroughly. Not easy yet about Jessie's safety, he had discreetly followed her and the Frenchman on deck and had kept out of sight in the shadows, watching the couple, listening to them talk—but, more to his purpose, keeping close watch over all the poopdeck.

Jessie and the Frenchman stood at the rail, a little forward of the mizzenmast. Behind them was the skylight that let daylight into the dining room and saloon below. At night the skylight was aglow with the yellow light from lamps in that large cabin, and that light fell on the couple at the rail. To keep out of sight, Ki stood at the opposite rail, in the shadow of the wheelhouse. He was alert, but the night was filled with sounds—shouting on the quay below, the snorting of draft horses, the incessant groaning of the ship's rigging—which overpowered the small sounds he wanted to hear.

Jessie was charmed by the Frenchman, so much so that Ki judged it likely that Henri Derval would share her cabin on this voyage. Jessie was an earthy young woman, appreciative of the pleasures of the flesh, yet realistic and controlled in her indulgence in those pleasures. She was no romantic, though even if she had been inclined toward such impulses, her life had left her little opportunity to indulge in fantasies.

A heavy thud. Close by. There was no one on the poop-deck but Jessie and the Frenchman and himself, and yet—His eyes searched the shadows. No one. Then, suddenly, it was clear to him—someone had come through the rigging and dropped to the roof of the wheelhouse. Ki leaped to the rail, then to the wheelhouse roof. Too late! Just as he landed on the roof, crouched to spring, a man dressed all in black leaped from the roof toward Jessie and the Frenchman, the steel blade in his hand glinting in the dim light.

All Ki could do was shout a warning. *"Jessie!"*

His shout gave the Frenchman the instant he needed to spring between Jessie and the man with the knife. Henri Derval caught the force of the man's assault and for a moment blunted it. But only for a moment. The attacker was small and wiry, and he easily threw the Frenchman aside. Derval fell to the deck, and the attacker turned toward Jessie, drawing back his knife for a thrust to her heart.

Ki sprang across the roof of the wheelhouse and poised on the far edge. He was grateful for the moment Henri Derval had given him, though he doubted it would be enough.

There was a loud *pop!* The attacker stood, shocked. He coughed.

Jessie's skirts were up to her hips. Her derringer was in her hand. She had shot the attacker once, in the belly, and she held the little pistol ready to fire its second barrel if the man did not fall.

The Frenchman jumped up from the deck. He grabbed the attacker by the wrist and pushed him against the rail. The attacker raised his knife against the Frenchman, and Derval hit him with a fist, so hard that the man's nose flattened against his face, crushed. Derval lunged against the attacker then, and upset him backward over the ship's rail. The man fell and splashed into the water below.

"I see no reason to report the matter to anyone," Jessie said a few minutes later, as they sat down in her cabin to discuss what had happened.

"I would rather be silent on the matter," said Henri. "Your government could delay me for some time while it investigates."

"There's nothing to investigate, as far as I'm concerned," said Jessie.

"Let us regard the matter as settled," said Ki. He had not sat down. "I will sleep with my cabin door open." He bowed and closed the door behind him as he left.

"You are remarkable people," said Henri. "You and Ki. I had heard you were, but..."

"I am grateful to you, Henri," said Jessie. "You threw yourself between me and that man. You could have been killed."

"I am afraid I was not very effective," said Henri.

"Effective enough," she said. "You gave me time to get to my derringer."

"Ah, yes," said Henri with a smile.

"Which reminds me," said Jessie. She lifted her skirt and pulled the derringer from the garter holster. Her stockings were gray, to match her dress, and above the stockings her thighs were bare. She reached for a box of cartridges, which lay at hand in her open trunk, and reloaded the derringer. "Here," she said, tossing the empty casing to Henri. "Souvenir."

He was staring at her legs and let the cartridge fall to the carpet.

Jessica tipped her head and regarded him quizzically. "You like my legs, Henri?"

He exhaled a loud sigh. *"Mais certainement,"* he said.

"You stared down into my dress when we danced. Did you like what you saw then, too?"

"I'm sorry," he said quickly. "Crude of me..."

She shook her head. "I would have been disappointed if you hadn't. I like to be reminded from time to time that

18

I'm something besides the head of the Starbuck empire, something besides a woman who can ride and shoot and fight."

"You *are* more," he said.

"I haven't the luxury of playing the coy little girl, Henri. I don't have the time. When I see a man I like, I have to let him know. I like you."

"I am . . . honored," he breathed.

Jessie smiled. "You have your cue. Do you require more?"

He stood, and she stood facing him. He drew her into his arms and pressed his mouth hard against hers. His mouth was open, and his tongue pressed against her lips and teeth. She opened her mouth and let his tongue inside, and their tongues sought each other urgently. She felt his erection swelling against her, and slipped her hand between their hips to feel his hard, growing shaft. He was big. She swelled with breath, in anticipation of how he would fill her.

Henri's hands worked feverishly at her back, unhooking the gray silk dress. He knew, of course, that she was wearing nothing under it, and when he had loosened it he stepped back from her and let it fall. Except for her shoes and stockings—and the little garter holster—she was naked. He held her at arm's length and stared at her breasts, smooth and pale and high.

Her face was flushed, not with embarrassment over her nakedness, but in excitement, in anticipation. "You too, Henri," she whispered. "You too. I want to see every inch of you."

He needed a minute to undress, and as he undressed she unhooked her holster and put it aside. She poured a splash of his brandy into one glass for them to share. She watched him. He was a well-built man, hard and taut. His male organ was bigger than her quick feel had suggested—long and thick, standing out in front of him like the ship's bowsprit.

He took her hand and led her, not to the narrow bed but to the leather-covered settee under the wide window at the rear of the cabin. *"Cherie,"* he whispered, "would you like to learn a few French tricks of love?"

Jessie smiled. "I am always interested in broadening my education."

"Most American women are afraid to learn."

"Perhaps I should tell you," Jessie said, "Ki is not the only Japanese who came to Texas with my father. There is another, a wonderful woman, a geisha, who has been my friend and teacher."

"Geisha," said Henri. "I've heard of them."

"The word means 'artist,'" said Jessie. "An artist of pleasure. She was trained in all the arts of pleasure: good food, good drink, good music, good conversation—and of course all the arts of love."

"You have perhaps something to teach me, then," suggested Henri.

"Perhaps," said Jessie. "If I know ten percent of all that Myobu knows..."

"Myobu?"

"Myobu, the geisha. You say American women are afraid to learn, but few American men are interested in a woman's pleasure. They hurry too much, take their pleasure, and leave their women dissatisfied."

"I won't do that to you, Jessie. Lie back. Are you able to cross your ankles behind your head? Few women can."

She laughed. Her young, slender body was supple; and easily, pulling each ankle up with her hand, she crossed them behind the back of her neck. It was a comfortable position, once she had attained it—and it put her womanly parts dramatically on display. He arranged cushions behind her back to assure her comfort. Wetting a finger with his tongue, he slipped a finger inside her, found her clitoris, and began gently to caress it.

Jessie was electrified. Her breath came short, she was aware that her whole body was flushing pink, and she moaned. He dipped a finger in brandy and rubbed it, not on her sensitive inner flesh, but on the outside, in her pubic hair. The brandy warmed her. He bent down and licked it off.

Twice more he spread brandy on her outer labia, warming them, then licking off the liquor. Each time his tongue

20

intruded farther into her, rough and mobile, stimulating the sensitive inner flesh. She writhed. He began to lick her then, starting his strokes at the bottom and licking upward. Her sensations deepened. At first, though she thrust herself forward to suggest it, he did not touch her clitoris with his tongue. Then he did, slightly. Then he did it more, at the top of each long stroke of his tongue through her warm, wet valley. She could anticipate it in his rhythm, and it was as if everything in her rose in anticipation of that touch. When finally he settled his mouth on her and gave his tongue exclusively to her clitoris, she surged into an immediate orgasm so intense that it was almost frightening.

He sat up and took a sip of brandy. She moved to slip an ankle from behind her neck, but he shook his head. He sat a little apart from her now and, with his right hand, caressed her breasts while with the fingers of his left he rubbed her inside parts, more vigorously than before, until in a little more than a minute she came to another, different climax.

"Henri . . ." she whispered. She pointed at his erect shaft. It was throbbing, engorged with blood.

He nodded. "Please."

She slipped her ankles from behind her neck and pressed him down on his back on the settee. She lifted first his stiff organ, then the sac beneath it, in her right hand, hefting them as if to feel their weight. They were hot. With gestures she encouraged him to pile the cushions under his hips, to lift his pelvis toward her, and to spread his legs as wide as he could, to offer his parts to her mouth. She bent down and licked him. Very gently she sucked on the loose, wrinkled skin of his scrotum, drawing first one testicle and then the other up to her lips. She lifted the fleshy bag out of the way and licked the place where it joined his body.

Now she took his shaft in her hands and rolled it between them. She accepted it into her mouth, as deeply into her throat as it would go, then pulled it out between tight lips. She felt his body stiffen.

Clutching his massive rod in her fist, she squeezed his foreskin up into a flower, and pressed her tongue into that flower. She set up a circular motion then, rubbing the sensitive foreskin with her wet tongue, touching the sensitive flesh concealed inside it only with the pointed tip. She kept her fingers tight around the shaft. Now and again she drew the foreskin between her lips and nibbled it.

As she had thought, he couldn't last long. His climax burst into her mouth. It continued an amazingly long time, pumping and pumping, until her mouth overflowed with his fluid, and she let it run out over her chin.

She sat up, grinning down at him. "You men," she said gently. "What a mess you make."

He offered her a silk handkerchief dipped in brandy, and she wiped her face. They kissed then. They sat clasped in each other's arms and kissed for a long time.

"Still," he said after a while, "as good as it is, what of this is geisha teaching?"

Jessie drew a breath. "I had supposed we had hardly begun," she said. She grinned at him. "All right. A little geisha trick, taught me by Myobu . . ."

She went to her trunk and returned in a moment carrying a pair of thongs, one of silk, one of thin, oiled rawhide. Though Henri drew back at first, she knotted them expertly around his shaft and tied them tight, circling and crisscrossing his length. "It's called *higozuiki,*" she told him. You'll stay stiff all night. And I . . . ah, with those on it, slipping in and out of me . . . But don't you learn this in France?"

★

Chapter 3

The *Sarah,* never more than two days out of sight of land, took twenty-two days to make the voyage from New Orleans to Veracruz. She put in twice en route, at Galveston Bay and Tampico, to discharge and take on passengers, unload and take on cargo. The trip was uneventful. Except for one small storm, in which the *Sarah* pitched and rolled alarmingly for two hours, the weather was good. The wind held, and the captain told Jessica proudly that they were making good time.

She spent much of her time on deck, not keeping to the poop as the other passengers were required to do, but strolling the length of the ship, exchanging pleasantries with the sailors, watching and learning the complicated business of working a sailing ship. She was one of only three women on board. The others, the wife and daughter of a former Republican congressman newly appointed to the post of senior counsel at the United States embassy in Mexico City, kept to their cabins and the saloon most of the time. The congressman and his wife were scandalized by Jessica's blue jeans and the display of her bosom in her tight checkered

23

shirt—which she did not button to the collar—and they seemed resolved to speak to her only when she was dressed for dinner. Baron Otto vom und zum Heligendorf sweated heavily in the tropical heat into which they were sailing on their southerly course, and his white suits hung damp and wrinkled from his portly frame. Except for his frequent nervous strolls on the poopdeck, he too kept mostly to his cabin and the saloon. As often as not, he did not appear for meals but asked that food, and invariably a bottle of brandy, be sent to his cabin.

Except that it took three weeks, during which time she was out of touch with everything happening among the varied Starbuck enterprises, Jessie enjoyed the ocean voyage.

Ki was stoically patient. He spent much of his time studying their fellow passengers, looking for the pair of eyes that had stared at him from behind the grinning mask on Mardi Gras night. He wondered if those eyes might not have belonged to the man Derval threw overboard into the Mississippi the night they sailed. Ki and Jessie had each killed a man in New Orleans—assuming it was her shot from the derringer that did in the man the Frenchman dumped over the rail—and Ki wondered if someone who employed both of them might not be among the passengers on this voyage.

As he customarily did when he had time on his hands, Ki spent hours with his weapons, checking, honing, oiling—and concealing. He wore a black leather vest, old and unprepossessing, and in its hidden pockets he could and did hide a score of *shuriken*, his throwing blades. What seemed to be a twisted rope belt to hold up his pants was in fact a *surushin*, a strong thin cord tipped at both ends with lead weights—a deadly weapon to a man who knew how to use it. In his baggage he carried his noble *katana*, the samurai sword left to him by his teacher after the old man committed *seppuku*. Ki almost never used it, but he treasured it. He had with him his bow and an assortment of arrows, including some of the "death's song" arrows, which emitted an eerie low whistle as they flew. He had an assortment of *nunchaku*

24

in several sizes—pairs of heavy sticks attached to each other by a horsehair link, that were bone-crushing weapons in his hands. Finally, he carried his *bo*, the five-foot staff he could use in so many varied ways.

On deck, ever alert, Ki wore his leather vest and went barefoot. He came to the table at night dressed in suit, vest, shirt, necktie, and Wellington boots. Only Jessie knew—and Henri suspected—that he was as heavily armed as if he had strolled the decks or sat at dinner with two Peacemakers strapped to his hips, a bowie knife stuck in his belt, and two or three derringers hidden here and there on his person. What Jessie also knew, and Henri did not yet suspect, was that Ki was almost as effective a fighting man without his weapons as he was with them.

The ex-congressman and his overweight wife scorned Ki as an Oriental. Their blond daughter, eighteen years old, was more perceptive than they and was fascinated by the lithe, dark figure who wore no shoes on deck and sometimes no shirt under his leather vest. She had never before seen a man with muscles like wire ropes and black eyes so deep and piercing. Her name was Susan McPherson, and Ki saw her fascination and pointedly kept clear of her until, after they had been at sea a week, he noticed that her father, almost alone of the passengers, visited the baron's cabin and seemed to engage in earnest conferences with him there. Seeing that, he allowed the girl to approach. Sensing that her mother or father would forbid her to speak with him if they saw her doing so, he found occasion to talk with her when her parents were out of sight. Before long they were exchanging signals, arranging on the instant small occasions to meet and talk.

She came to his cabin. It was the first officer's cabin, more spacious than most of the passenger cabins, and he had two chairs and a small table as well as his bunk. Susan was interested in his Japanese ancestry and in things Japanese generally. He talked at length with her and finally was able to lead the conversation to her father and to his apparent friendship with the baron.

"Mexico!" the girl said with a sneer. "We were promised Paris. Or maybe London. Vienna, at least, or Rome."

"Promised?" Ki asked.

"Promised," she said. "By Mr. Blaine. And Mr. Frelinghuysen confirmed it when he became Secretary of State."

"Promised, in return for what?"

"I'm not sure," said Susan. "It was something my father could help them do—as a congressman, I mean."

"And what did the baron have to do with it?" Ki asked.

"It's the baron who got us stuck in Mexico," she said. "He's promised we go on to Paris from Mexico, but I don't trust him."

"Political deal," Ki said with a smile, as if to dismiss the subject.

"Yes. All my life I've had to listen to them talk about their political deals. Beef, wheat, coal, iron, sugar."

"Sugar?" Ki asked.

She nodded. "Sugar. Someday, they say, you won't be able to put sugar in your coffee unless you buy it from them. The whole world market. No one will have any sugar but them."

"Interesting," Ki mused. "An interesting idea."

Susan learned to marvel over, and to trust, his superior hearing and instincts; and she became willing to enter his cabin on his assurance that no one was in the corridor, no one about to turn a corner, no one to see her come or go. Always, before he let her enter, he checked carefully. The cabin doors were louvered, and he could hear every sound in the passageway. Susan learned quickly to feel secure with him.

He felt less than secure with her. She was young and inexperienced. He feared she would form an attachment to him if he indulged in any intimacy with her. She suggested by girlish signs that she wanted him to kiss her, maybe even to do more; but he smiled on her, treated her like a sister, and let her enjoy the excitement she found in clandestine meetings. The last time she was in his cabin, as their ship beat into the harbor at Veracruz, she asked him to kiss her, and he gave her a light, brotherly kiss—not enough, he

26

hoped, to encourage her to greater boldness, but still enough to remember.

He said nothing to Jessie about the scheme to monopolize the world's trade in sugar. He mulled it over in his mind, and it seemed too remote from the problem they had come to Veracruz to solve.

Veracruz was like a score of other towns that Jessie and Ki had seen—small, torpid, squalid, oppressed. That it was in Mexico and not in the Rio Grande country of southern Texas was evident only in the damp, unrelieved heat, the lush greenery, and the character of the people in the streets. It was a port town, and every nationality was represented here; but the Mexicans were Indians, Mayans, tall and full-lipped and dark. Like any other Mexican town, Veracruz was built around its churches—high, white, brooding, ancient. Priests and monks strode along the streets, hurrying on God's business. They shouldered their way through knots of drunken sailors, past whores lounging in doorways even in midday. Wagons and carts lumbered through the dust, carrying goods to and from the docks. There seemed to be no siesta in Veracruz. Tropical though the town was, it was busy.

Accompanied by Henri Derval, Jessie and Ki walked the short distance from the dock to the Hotel Real, where the *hotelero* knew the name Starbuck and pronounced himself honored to receive Señorita Starbuck as a guest. Their three adjoining rooms overlooked a quiet stone courtyard and garden, where birds splashed in the bowl of a fountain and huge red flowers sent up a cloyingly sweet odor.

They agreed to meet Henri Derval for dinner, and shortly after noon, Jessie and Ki left the hotel to walk to the Veracruz office of Starbuck Shipping.

With instructions from the *hotelero*, they were easily able to find the street where the office was located, within sight of the waterfront, of course. It was also a street lined with bars and bordellos and populated with all the scum that preyed on the sailors coming ashore from the ships, their pockets laden with wages that they were all too eager to

27

squander on the diversions that such a port city had to offer. Jessie saw Ki tense up as they entered the street. In a moment he had reason.

"'Ey, Señorita!"

The leering calls came from all sides, not from the sailors but from oily men who prowled among them—procurers. They seemed to think they saw in Jessica, maybe in her tight blue jeans and shirt, a recruit for their commerce. It would have been possible perhaps to walk through them, except that one, maybe a little drunk, chose to come near and grab her arm. He was a big man, more than six feet tall and heavy, wearing loose white clothing. His hand closed around her arm and jerked her off balance. He growled a few words in Spanish. She had no idea what the words were, but she knew she was hearing a demand, not a proposition.

Ki moved as quickly as the striking of a rattler, yet controlled, with force enough to shatter the man's nose. The hardened heel of Ki's hand struck like the square side of a blade, with the sickening crack of breaking bone and cartilage, and in the same instant it was withdrawn and ready to strike again.

The man staggered back, clutching his nose, blood oozing from between his fingers. For a moment he glared at Ki, dazed; then a scowl spread over his face, replaced quickly by an ugly grin. "Ah, chino," he grunted. "Bastardo." From beneath his shirt he drew a knife.

In a moment it was apparent the man was an experienced knife fighter. He spread his feet and circled Ki, bouncing on the balls of his feet, remarkably agile for so big and heavy a man.

The street fell silent and a crowd formed, making a wide ring around Ki and Jessie and the white-clad man with the knife. Jessie searched the crowd for some sign of an officer of the law. She knew Ki could launch a *shuriken* at any time he chose and kill the man on the spot, but she was not sure how this crowd, on this street, would react—or how Veracruz law would react. Ki seemed relaxed enough. He

28

turned and kept his face to the bouncing, circling man, but he made no move.

"Ho! Alto!"

A priest in a black cassock broke through the crowd. He was a tall, thin young man with a fringe of black beard along his jawline. He strode into the open space in the middle of the crowd, with the air of a man accustomed to authority and deference.

"Norteamericanos?" he asked Jessica.

"Yes, Father. The man grabbed me. My friend is trying to protect me."

The priest faced the man with the knife. *"Basta!"* he snapped, and with a peremptory gesture ordered the man away.

The man shook his head and muttered to himself.

The priest stepped closer to him, and the man suddenly swung with his left hand and struck the priest full in the face. The young priest fell in the dust. The man with the knife turned again to Ki, his grin spreading, his eyes glittering.

"Run, Chinaman," the priest yelled at Ki. "He will kill you. He has killed before." He struggled to his knees. "Run!"

Ki stood his ground, and the man moved toward him, arms wide. He came slowly for a step or two, then lurched forward. He was fast. Ki was faster. Ki stepped aside and launched himself into a *yoko-geri-keage*—a sideways snap-kick. Cocking his leg to gain the utmost force, he slashed out with his calloused foot. The tremendous kick smashed into the man's kneecap. The kneecap shattered and the man fell to the ground, howling, crippled for life. In his agony he dropped his knife and rolled in the dust, clutching his leg and screaming. He did not try to rise. He could not have. He leg was useless and would never work properly again.

The crowd did not understand how badly the procurer was injured, only that a bully who had cowed them all was rolling in the dust and shrieking, and they began to laugh.

The priest stood, brushing the dust from his cassock.

"So," he said to Ki. "Japanese, then? We know of you."

"We know of you, Father," said Ki calmly. "The Jesuits and the Japanese have a long friendship."

The priest glanced at the procurer, who was still rolling in the dust. "You have done our community a service," he said dryly.

"My name is Jessica Starbuck," said Jessie. "This is Ki."

"Your office is there, Miss Starbuck," said the priest, pointing to a wooden building across the street. "It is unfortunate you have to come to this street. If you come again, I suggest you come dressed as a lady. My name is Father Roberto."

Jessica smiled. "Thank you, Father."

"Go with God," said the priest as he turned away.

The Starbuck manager in Veracruz was a former Confederate naval officer named Andrew Bragg. Jessica knew his history. She had checked it in her father's records before she decided to voyage to Veracruz. He had operated first as a blockade runner, then as a privateer. After Appomattox the federal government had for a time regarded him as a felon, and he had fled to Veracruz. When Alex Starbuck encountered him, Bragg had run out of funds and was desperate for honest employment. Starbuck had hired him and secured him a full pardon from President Grant. Bragg had married here in Veracruz, to a Mexican girl of Spanish-Mayan ancestry. When Alex Starbuck subsequently offered him a job in San Francisco, Bragg had replied he would rather stay in Veracruz.

Jessie decided immediately on seeing him that Andrew Bragg drank too much. His swollen nose was marked with violet veins, his face was red, he was softly overweight, and his bulging blue eyes were moist. He had adapted himself to the tropics and faced her in his second-floor office, wearing the white cotton trousers and loose white cotton shirt that were so common on the street.

"I was anxious about you, Miss Starbuck," he said. "I didn't know you were coming until Captain Baldwin came in and said you had sailed from New Orleans with him on

30

the *Sarah*. I'm pleased that you've found good accommodations, though I hope you will move to my home and regard it as yours for the duration of your stay."

"Thank you, but we will stay at the hotel," said Jessie. "Ki and I are apt to discommode people considerably with our sudden changes of plan."

"You've come about the *Abraham,* of course," said Bragg.

"That and the three other ships," said Jessica.

"Yes. Yes, of course," said Bragg. He pointed to a huge map of the Gulf of Mexico, which covered almost all of one wall of his office. "Coming down from Tampico, they hardly leave sight of land. They're taken within twenty miles of the coast. They just disappear. It's as if they're captured by ghosts, Miss Starbuck. In fact, that's what they say in Veracruz, that the Starbuck ships are being attacked by ghost pirates."

"We, of course, know better," said Jessie.

"Of course," agreed Bragg. "Of course."

"What have you done to investigate?" Ki asked.

"The law here is represented by Don Perfecto Morelos, the governor of Veracruz. He has extended every cooperation."

"We should see him, I suppose," said Jessica.

Bragg shook his head. "Veracruz is a big province, Miss Starbuck. It extends from Tampico to Coatzacoalcos, more than six hundred miles. The governor is now, I believe, in Jalapa."

"And with his cooperation, still you've learned nothing?" Jessica asked.

"We have not been idle, Miss Starbuck," said Bragg solemnly. "I have sent agents up and down the coast, looking for the lost ships. We believe they are not taken just for their cargo and sunk afterward, but that the men who are stealing them want the ships themselves. Until this week I was able to discover no trace either of the ships or their cargoes. Now I believe I have an idea where the Starbuck ships are being taken."

"Where, Mr. Bragg?"

Bragg stood and touched a spot on the map. "Here," he

said. "Bahía de Culebras. It means the Bay of Snakes. It is a cove, actually—an inlet surrounded by forested highlands. There is no fresh water there, so even fishing boats do not put in unless driven by a storm. I am by no means certain of the matter, but I have reason to believe the Starbuck ships are being taken there to be refitted."

"Refitted?"

"Yes," said Bragg. The effort of standing and pointing at the map had reddened his face, and beads of sweat stood on his forehead. "Changed. So they will not be readily recognized. Rerigged. Painted." He nodded. "They will return to sea as someone else's ships."

"What makes you think the ships are being refitted in this bay?" Jessica asked.

"I have sent agents up and down the coast, offering bribes to anyone, officials especially, who can give me information about the missing ships. Until now their reports have been few and sparse. But this week I received a report from an agent in Jalapa. He paid a captain of *rurales* to ride the coastline for fifty miles, looking into every slightest inlet. The captain, he reports, says he saw two large ships in the Bahía de Culebras. They may not be the missing Starbuck ships, but—"

"What have you done about it?"

"I have sent a courier to the governor. The governor will send troops to investigate."

"How long will it take for the troops to arrive there?" Ki asked.

"The courier will require a few days to reach the governor. Travel is not easy in this country, Miss Starbuck. Then, if the governor—"

"If?"

Bragg nodded. "If the governor has troops available and elects to send them, they will require perhaps another week to reach the bay."

"By which time the ships may be gone," said Jessie impatiently.

"Exactly. And that is why I am also sending a party of

our own, a few men, to look into the bay and at least identify the ships there."

"And what if they find them?" Jessica asked. "Will they try to recapture them?"

Bragg shook his head. "They will require help. The pirates must number fifty men or more, to have seized our ships, to have sailed them to the Bay of Snakes, to be refitting them."

"Has your party left Veracruz yet?" Jessica asked.

"No. I am assembling them."

"If all they are to do is look, they need not go. I will go myself. I want to see these pirates."

"That will be quite impossible, Miss Starbuck."

"Oh? Why?"

"This country—there are bandits on the roads. The *rurales*—the provincial soldiers—are not always friendly. They operate quite independently sometimes. It is rough country between here and the Bahía de Culebras. It will be hot." Bragg shook his head emphatically. "You would require horses. A carriage. A wagon for your tents and other gear. The carriage and wagon will attract thieves. You would need a party of soldiers to accompany you."

"Well, if Ki and I don't go out of town at the head of a brass band, trumpeting to everyone that some rich Americans are traveling north, we might manage to go sixty miles without all these bandits and renegade soldiers knowing who we are, or where."

"But your supplies," Bragg protested. "You will find no inns, nowhere to eat or sleep."

"Ki and I are accustomed to traveling light, Mr. Bragg," said Jessica. "And sometimes we travel very fast. It has been to our advantage more than once."

"You don't even speak Spanish!"

Jessie nodded. "I will require an interpreter, someone you trust absolutely—and if he can use a gun, so much the better. Three riding horses, a packhorse, some beans, coffee—you know. We have our own guns and ammunition."

Openmouthed, Bragg shook his head. "But, Miss—"

"I will require all this at the Hotel Real at dawn, Mr. Bragg. We will leave at dawn. Would you care to come?"

"Oh—I fear not, Miss Starbuck."

Jessica nodded and rose from her chair. "At dawn, Mr. Bragg," she said firmly.

Chapter 4

Jessie was satisfied with what Bragg provided, including the interpreter. Everything was on the street in front of the hotel at dawn, when they came out after a Texas-style breakfast arranged at her special order by the *hotelero*. She swung up into the saddle of the chestnut mare Bragg had sent for her, and as their little party—Jessica, Ki, the interpreter, one packhorse laden with gear—turned north and set out through the town for the road north, they saw a different Veracruz. For once it was quiet. The dust was laid and everything glistened damply from a heavy dew. The light of dawn lent a charming rosy glow even to the city's most squalid shacks. They scattered flocks of chickens in the streets, and they had to ride around pigs lazing in the cool morning air. The smell of the salt sea merged with the sweet odors of tropical flowers. It was not so difficult to understand, at this hour, why Andrew Bragg had chosen to remain here, even when after he had been pardoned in the United States and could have returned there.

Over dinner in the hotel last night, Henri Derval had tried to talk her out of this venture. She had offered him, only half facetiously, the option of coming with her. If he felt she would not be safe, she said, he could come along and help Ki to protect her. Henri had smiled and said he doubted she would benefit much by another man's protection; she was eminently capable of protecting herself. But he argued that traveling by horseback along this coast could be dangerous even for ten or twenty armed men. She would not be dissuaded, and he dropped the subject.

Henri said he meant to conduct a little investigation of his own. Some of his wine, he said, might have shown up in Veracruz or elsewhere. While she went looking for ships, he would look for wine. The *Sarah,* he reminded her, would sail in three days for Havana and would return to Veracruz in about a month. It was his intention to return to New Orleans aboard the *Sarah,* and he hoped he would have the pleasure of her company on that voyage.

Baron Otto vom und zum Heligendorf had stopped by their table during dinner—to pay his respects, as he said. He told Jessie he had suffered a touch of seasickness all during their voyage from New Orleans and apologized for not having been more sociable aboard ship. It had been an honor, he said, to be aboard the *Sarah* with its charming owner. He had heard, he said, that she planned to travel north in search of her lost ships, and he cautioned her, as Henri had done, about the hazards of travel in Mexico. He returned then to his own table, where he was dining with Congressman McPherson and his wife and daughter.

The interpreter sent by Bragg was a tall, taciturn, middle-aged man of uncertain ancestry—he had the dark skin and full lips of the Mayan Indians of the vicinity, and perhaps he was in fact Mayan. He dressed, though, like a *norte-americano,* in a pair of rugged and well-worn blue jeans, with a gray shirt and a broad-brimmed Stetson. He carried a Remington Frontier .44 in a low-slung holster hung from a wide belt. He said his name was Ramondo, and on that subject he said nothing further, giving no hint whether Ramondo was his first name or last. In response to her question, he said he had worked for Starbuck Shipping for many years, but from the way he sat a horse, Jessie doubted he had spent much time at sea.

They soon left Veracruz behind and found themselves in country not much different from parts of Texas. It was different in that the sea was always to their right, sometimes out of sight through the tropical vegetation. To their left they could see distant mountains. The ground was sandy. The countryside was open, by no means forested, and usually they could see a mile or more around. To call the track they followed a road would have been an exaggeration. Most of the time it was hardly identifiable. If, in fact, Ramondo was following a track or simply leading them parallel to the coastline and far enough back to be on high ground and off the beach, she could not tell.

They passed through no villages worthy of the name. Every few miles they rode past a cluster of two or three houses, but Jessie decided a settlement would be defined as a place with a church, and they rode all morning without seeing a church. As the sun climbed higher they felt the heat more and more. Ramondo told them it would be wise to stop in the middle of the day, to take a meal and rest in the shade; the horses would need it even if they didn't, and they could ride on into the evening if Miss Starbuck wished.

Ki found it difficult to retain and establish that degree of alertness he considered necessary in the circumstances. The primitive road, the nearness and smell of the sea, the looming presence of distant mountains, the smell of blossoms from nearby groves, turned his mind to a similar slow ride along a seaside road on the Japanese island of Kyushu, many years ago. Very young then, he had not yet encountered the man who would make the most favorable impression on him of any man he had met in his life—Alex Starbuck. He had sought his fortune in his own country at first, never dreaming that fate would soon carry him far from home, to a distant continent called North America.

It troubled Ki that the baron knew they were traveling north. It could only mean that Andrew Bragg was not especially circumspect—no great surprise—but Ki wondered if it meant more. If it meant more, why had the baron mentioned his knowledge? For that matter, why had the baron troubled himself to come to their table and speak with Jessie at all? Was it possible the baron was nothing but a fat Prussian arms merchant, possessing no motives potentially threatening to the Starbuck name and enterprises?

Ki was troubled also by an impression—thus far unconfirmed by any observation—that they were being followed or watched. He was satisfied that their encounter on the street with the drunken procurer of whores had been an unfortunate chance, unrelated to the two attempts on Jessie's life in New Orleans. On the other hand, whoever had attempted to kill her there had to be somewhere—and it was unlikely they had left all threats behind in Louisiana.

He was more comfortable with the heat of approaching midday than Jessie or Ramondo could be. He wore his loose old leather vest directly over his shoulders, with no shirt. His feet were bare. Whatever breeze cooled them also cooled him. Jessie had opened all the top buttons of her shirt, to let the air in and around her breasts, but she sweated under her brown Stetson, and perspiration ran into her eyes. Ki wore a bandanna wrapped around his forehead, for the very purpose of blocking the flow of sweat into his eyes, but it was a sensible Japanese custom that even Jessie had not elected to adopt.

Ramondo led them at about noon into the poor little square of a tiny Mexican village. A small church, without a spire or bell, fronted the square and its fountain—actually just a small stone basin into which water trickled from a corroded pipe. The priest, an old, palsied man with a fringe of gray beard, greeted them at the door of his church and invited them to water their horses at the fountain. The square was all but abandoned. The men, Ki supposed, were at work in the surrounding fields, as were most of the women. The children too young to work—including, to Ki's surprise, girls perhaps as old as fourteen—played naked in the square. Besides the church, none of the buildings and houses were solid. The poverty of the place utterly shouted from its squalid fronts.

Still, it had its modest beauty. They settled near the

fountain in the shade of a low, lush tree. The horses drank. The old priest sat down on the ground and accepted Jessie's offer—communicated through Ramondo—to share their midday meal, particularly one of the bottles of Henri Derval's wine, which they had carried along in their saddlebags. The naked children gathered around and stared. The priest talked little. They could understand some of what he said; Ramondo translated the rest.

"He says there are ruins north of here, which you should see."

"What kind of ruins?" Jessie asked.

"From the very old time," Ramondo answered.

It was true. When, after two hours' rest in the shaded square, they rode on northward, they shortly came on a most amazing sight. At first the ancient ruins seemed nothing more than another small hill, overgrown with trees and brush. Then they recognized the pyramidal shape as too regular to be natural. They turned off the track and rode the few hundred yards to the base of the pyramid. It was, in fact, exactly that—a pyramid built of stones, perhaps a hundred feet high. It was covered with vegetation, including thick vines that clung to the worn, moss-covered stones; and the roots seemed to be gradually dislodging the stones and threatening the continued existence of the ancient structure. Venomous snakes slithered for cover as they approached.

"Of the old time," Ramondo said, nodding.

"Magnificent," said Jessica.

"Ah," Ramondo spat contemptuously. "It is nothing. There are some great ones. This one is but small. There were great cities, built of stone, around temples like this." He shook his head. "All gone now. All gone..."

They rode on. As their distance from Veracruz increased, the track gradually disappeared and they rode through open country, still parallel to the sea, still within sight of great mountains to the west, but abandoned. The poor farms became fewer, and they saw no one and no livestock. Ramondo was silent. He seemed to brood.

The more they were alone, the more it seemed to Ki they

39

were not alone. Still, he saw no sign. He searched the countryside for any evidence that they were followed or watched. Absolutely nothing suggested it, but the idea would not go away. When sunset came and Ramondo suggested they camp for the night, Ki rejected the campsite he suggested and looked for another one, more protected. He settled on a small strip of sandy beach protected by rocks. There, he calculated, they could choose a concealed campsite among the rocks, and a distant observer would not know exactly where they were.

Anyway, the sea was near, and Ki knew Jessie would appreciate that. In the brief southern twilight she stripped and plunged into the surf, to wash the sweat from her body. Ki sat on a rock and watched. Ramondo pretended to busy himself over their fire and not to look. Ki could not blame him if he did.

Ramondo slept as if there were nothing to fear. Jessie slept the first few hours and then rose and sat alert, apart from the fire, cradling her Winchester in her lap. Ki sat fully alert while she slept, then slipped into his controlled half-sleep during the hours she was on watch. In this way he could get his rest without surrendering his consciousness entirely, and he allowed the day's fatigue to drain from him fully, while he remained aware of every sound.

Well before dawn he rose and went to her. He told her to have another hour's sleep; he was rested and would stand watch the rest of the night. It was during that hour that his suspicions of the day before were confirmed. They were being watched. Someone was following. Someone, indeed, tried to slip into their camp.

If he had thought it was only a poverty-stricken Mexican coming to steal, he would have let the man go. But it was no poor Mexican. The man who came wore leather; he could hear it squeak. He heard the distinctive squeak of a leather belt, likely a gunbelt, also the different squeak of boots. The man was alone, unless he was accompanied by the quietest of trackers. Ki distinctly heard one man.

He had brought his bow to his lookout post, thinking he might have the chance to shoot a fat hare or a bird for their

40

breakfast, and he had a quiver of assorted arrows. He slipped off the rock where he had sat and slipped silently to another rock; the intruder, if he was clever, might have discovered his place before he sneaked toward the camp. Ki checked the faint moon. It would emerge from behind a wisp of cloud in a moment, offering enough light for him to see a little better. Actually, he didn't need to see. He could hear. The man came nearer.

Still, he was fifty yards away when the moonlight brightened a bit and Ki caught sight of him. He had not yet decided what to do about the man, but what he saw in the moment of dim moonlight decided that question. The man was a North American or a European, blond, slight, dressed in black—a black suit, with a cravat at his throat, strange dress for the time and place. He wore a gunbelt outside his coat, pinching it in, but the pistol was in place in its holster. The man carried something in his hand, a bundle of sticks...

Sticks of dynamite!

Ki watched. The man was clever, careful, experienced. A watcher without Ki's years of training, without his keenly sharpened senses, would never have heard him or seen him. He had come in the last hour before dawn, when people slept most soundly, when a lookout would most likely doze or at least his senses would be dulled. He came alone, professional and confident.

For a moment Ki considered his options. He could kill the man easily, with one of his razor-sharp barbed arrows. At this distance he could put an arrow through the man's throat, or into his heart. And if he did, whoever was behind him would send another man, then another. Ki decided that, for now at least, he would send a warning. An emphatic warning.

He waited only for the man to pause to listen, to peer into the darkness, to judge the likely whereabouts of the camp into which he meant to throw his deadly bundle of dynamite. In that moment, as the man stood still, Ki drew a cleaver arrow—one with a broad rectangular head, meant originally for cutting down an enemy's standard, used also for cutting ropes and harness. In a single motion he notched his arrow and drew it all the way behind his ear. He was a master of *kyujutsu,* the technique of bow and arrow, at which his teacher had compelled him to practice endlessly, for years; to an untrained eye it would have seemed he did not even aim. The arrow flew with a faint whisper on the air, straight to the wrist of the hand in which the man held the dynamite. In effect, it amputated the hand. It severed bone and muscle, leaving the hand hanging by a cord of bleeding flesh.

The man did not scream. He stiffened, then bent over, staring at the stump of his arm and the nearly severed hand. As Ki watched, grimly fascinated, the man retained the presence of mind to seize his arm in his remaining hand, squeezing hard to stop the flow of blood as best he could; and, though Ki could hear his shuddering breath, the man still retained control sufficient to retreat, to run back the way he had come—probably confident that his confederates, and help, were not too far away. Ki could not help admiring him. This had been a brave man, a worthy and dangerous foe. Ki wondered how many like him waited in the dark.

They broke camp at dawn. Ki insisted they ride a mile or so along the beach before mounting to higher ground. It was slow going, through the sand, sometimes with the surf reaching their horses' hooves, and among the seaside rocks, but it avoided any trap that might have been set for them above. Ramondo observed and kept quiet. If he had any suspicion that their camp had been approached just before dawn or that professional assassins waited somewhere, he showed no sign.

Ki had not told Jessie about the man with the bomb. He didn't have to. Though she did not know who had approached and how Ki had dealt with him, she knew something had happened in the night. She checked her pistol—the .38-caliber Colt on the .44 frame that her father had ordered specially made for her years ago.

This day was as bright and hot as the one before. With luck they might reach the area of the Bahía de Culebras by nightfall. But they would not approach the inlet tonight in any case, she and Ki had decided. They would make a careful approach sometime tomorrow, after they had reconnoitered.

When the sun was high, the trail disappeared. Though their course was evident—simply northward, parallel to the coast—Ramondo trotted ahead some fifty yards, up a small rise, and paused there, peering around as if looking for the way. He sat there for a moment on his horse, looking back at them; then suddenly he spurred and slapped his horse and galloped off to the north and west, over the crest of the rise and beyond, out of sight.

"Down!" Ki yelled at Jessica, throwing himself off his horse and grabbing the reins of hers.

She tumbled off just as she heard the shots. The bullets whistled past above her horse, where she would have been sitting now, but for Ki's shout. He ran, and she followed. They ran toward the beach, which here was no more than twenty yards from them. With bullets snapping around them, Jessie and Ki jumped over the edge of a short drop and landed on the sand below.

Their attackers were determined, and were no cowards. They came on, charging toward them on horseback, at least five of them. Jessie and Ki raised themselves to look over the lip of the drop, to see exactly where the horsemen were, and found to their surprise that the horses were coming full speed directly at them, the riders firing ahead. Jessie and Ki threw themselves down to avoid being trampled, and the horses and riders jumped over them, thudding down just behind them on the sand.

Rolling over, Jessie faced six of them, not five, leveling their weapons, taking deadly aim. She saw the flash of a *shuriken* already flying toward their attackers. Her Colt was in her hand, and she fired almost before she aimed, at the nearest horseman. A bullet kicked up sand beside her leg, and she fired again.

One man slumped in his saddle. Another grabbed his throat. Still another, though, spurred his horse toward them. Ki leaped to his feet and threw his body into the air, aiming a kick at the horse's neck. The creature screamed and reared as the powerful kick broke into its breath, and its rider's pistol shot went into the air. Jessie shot a man who was taking aim on Ki. Leaping again, Ki drove a powerful sideways blow with his arm into the ribs of the man on the rearing horse. Ribs broke, and the man lost his grip on the horse and slipped to the ground.

Abruptly the attack was over. Four of the attackers retreated. One lay dead. The man with broken ribs ran a few steps after his panicked horse, then stumbled and fell.

Jessie walked over to him. She bent over him and took his pistol from his limp hand.

"Look at this," she said to Ki.

Ki looked and nodded. The pistol was a Mauser, a European make rarely seen on this side of the Atlantic. The man himself was European, to judge from the look of his clothes. He wore khaki breeches and cavalry boots, a white shirt with a necktie, and a khaki jacket. He had a thin red mustache and sandy red hair. His sweating face was flushed.

"Do you speak English?" Jessie asked.

The man didn't answer.

Jessie glanced around. "Well, your horse has run off. We can leave you here."

The man lay on his back and watched them round up their own horses. Jessie's mare turned out to be well trained and had run only far enough to be out of danger. When Jessie spotted her and whistled, the mare trotted up. She remounted and soon recovered Ki's mount and the packhorse. Ki lifted the European onto the packhorse. Within an hour they were moving again, slowly.

"It makes no difference that you won't tell us who you are," Jessie said to the European a little later. "We know, really. Or at least I think I know who you work for."

The man said nothing. The color was gone from his face. He concentrated on holding himself aboard the plodding packhorse.

They had ridden only another two or three miles when they heard the sound of many horses. They dismounted, and Jessie pulled her Winchester from its scabbard. The horsemen came from the west, as though from the mountains—twenty or more of them, immediately identifiable as Mexicans.

"Rurales," Jessie said to Ki as the horsemen drew up.

One of the horsemen, thinner and more erect than the rest, rode forward and saluted. Jessie remounted so she could speak directly with him.

"Please to understand," said the man, in heavily accented English. "I am Capitan Juan Vincente Ortiz. I hearby place the two of you—you, Señorita, and you, chino—in the arrest. Please to hand over your weapons."

"May I ask why we are arrested?" Jessie asked.

"For the murder," said the captain.

"Murder?" Jessie protested. "Of whom?"

"Two innocent men," said the captain. "And wound others—including this one." He pointed at the European on the packhorse.

"We were attacked!" Jessie cried angrily. "We only defended ourselves. Six of them attacked us!"

"Others describe the matter otherwise," said the captain. "Please. Your weapons."

They had no choice. The *rurales* knew nothing of Ki's *shuriken,* hidden in the pockets of his leather vest, but they took his bow. They did not search Jessie and did not find her derringer, but they took her Colt and Winchester. That they had overlooked weapons on their two prisoners made no difference. They had been warned of Ki's prowess, so they fastened his hands behind his back with a pair of huge and ancient manacles, and though they let her have her hands in front of her, they locked another pair on Jessie's wrists.

The captain shot a peremptory gesture to the west, and the *rurales* formed a column, riding away from the coast and toward the distant hills, away from the Bay of Snakes.

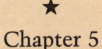

Chapter 5

La Paz de Cristo was a hill town, ten miles inland, built there and not on the coast apparently because the soil was better and springs provided a supply of fresh water. Sheep grazed on the hillsides as the column of *rurales* approached the town over a track that was no more than the suggestion of a road. La Paz de Cristo was large enough to have two churches, one with a tall steeple with a bell hanging in a high arch. It was market day, and the few short streets and the town square were noisy with the simple business of selling and buying. Everything seemed to be for sale — vegetables, fruits, animals, fowl, bread, clothes, tools, guns. A wine shop was doing brisk business, selling pots of red wine.

It was picturesque, but Jessie could not appreciate it. She sat slumped in her saddle, giddy with the unrelieved heat, damp all over with sweat, worried and afraid. The iron shackles were a heavy weight on her wrists, but she could move her arms much more than Ki could, and she was deeply concerned about him, with his hands locked behind his back. He rode stoically, glancing at her occasionally.

He had shown neither her nor the *rurales* any hint of emotion, and she wanted, more than anything, a moment alone to speak with him.

Her derringer was within reach under her belt, and Ki had probably a dozen *shuriken* at hand the moment his hands were freed; still, she wondered how they would fight twenty-five soldiers and maybe a whole village. She wondered if they should, or if maybe their best course would not be to rely on Mexican law. If the captain of these soldiers was in fact some kind of officer, as he said he was, then perhaps he would try to do justice. Maybe they should put some reliance on that. Maybe they had to.

She wondered who had accused her and Ki. Somehow it seemed out of character with the men who had attacked them, and the nature of the attack, that those men would go to the law. For them to recruit new forces and attack again would be consistent. For them to complain to Mexican authorities that *they* had been attacked and two of them murdered would not be.

The troop of *rurales* rode through a gate on the uphill side of the village square, into a large bare courtyard, where they dismounted. Giving orders in Spanish, the captain ordered a detail of his men to help the manacled prisoners to dismount and to lead them into the largest of the buildings that faced the courtyard. Jessie walked between two soldiers, one holding her by each arm. They led her into a cool, shadowed interior, along a corridor and through what appeared to be an anteroom to a larger chamber beyond. There, she and Ki were required to sit on a bench, under the eyes of four soldiers.

"How bad is this, do you think?" she asked Ki quietly.

He shook his head. "I think we will soon find out."

"Is there any escape?"

"There may have to be."

Captain Ortiz entered the room, knocked gently on the double doors that led to the next chamber, and was admitted to that room. Jessie had only a glimpse inside and could see only that it was indeed a big chamber, carpeted, paneled—the office, she judged, of the captain's superior.

After they had waited another quarter hour, the doors swung wide open, and the four soldiers led Jessie and Ki into the chamber. There a corpulent elderly man with a white beard sat behind a huge desk of dark wood. He was dressed in a gray suit of Prince Albert cut, with a vest and a heavy gold watch chain, and he wore pearl-gray kid gloves. Captain Ortiz stood respectfully to one side of him.

The white-bearded man spoke English, very good English. "I am Don Francisco Tolosa," he said. "I am *alcalde* here. If you do not know that term, it means I am, among other things, a judge."

"I am Jessica Starbuck," said Jessie. "I am a citizen of the United States."

"Yes, I know who you are, Miss Starbuck," Don Francisco replied.

"We are falsely accused," Jessie pressed on. "We rely on you, sir, to do justice."

"I intend to," said the *alcalde*. "Be seated, please."

She and Ki were seated in two chairs in the center of the floor, facing the big desk. They remained handcuffed. Four soldiers stood guard over them, one at each side and two behind their chairs.

"The charges against you," said the *alcalde*, "are that you murdered two men, to wit, one Kurt Zimmer and one Basilio Cardi. One died of some sort of blade that struck him in the throat, and the other of a bullet wound. Others were injured in what has been described to me as an attack by you and a certain Mexican in your employ, who escaped, on a party of businessmen traveling from Veracruz to Jalapa. Since you deny the charges, we will call in the witnesses and hear the evidence."

"Are we to understand we are on trial now?" Jessie asked.

The *alcalde* nodded. "I intend to dispose of the matter today," he said. He nodded to the captain. "The witnesses, please."

Captain Ortiz left the chamber through a side door and returned in a moment, bringing four men. Jessie gasped. One of them was the Baron Otto vom und zum Heligendorf!

The four men sat on a row of chairs along one side of

49

the room. One of them carried his right arm in a sling, and the heavy bandaging at his wrist indicated that he had recently lost his right hand. He was pallid and weak, but he glared at Ki with furious hatred. All four of the men were dressed in suits with vests and watch chains—the baron in a suit of white linen. The baron fixed his eyes on the *alcalde* and kept them away from Jessie.

"Now we know," she whispered to Ki.

He nodded.

At the suggestion of the *alcalde,* the man with his arm in a sling spoke first, in a heavy German accent:

"Ve vere on our horses riding, on our vay from Veracruz to Jalapa, ven suddenly ve vere attacked. Ze Japanner fired at me a very cruel arrow, vun viz a knife blade, vich struck me on mine arm und cut off mind hand. I—"

"The Japanese was carrying this bow and such arrows when I arrested him," said Captain Ortiz.

"Zey fired on us," the man continued. "Ze Japanner, ze voman, und ze tall Mexicaner. Ve vere surprised. It vas only after I had been so badly vounded and Kurt had been killed zat any of us fired back. I sink zey vould have killed us all, if some of us had not fired back."

"And do I understand," asked the *alcalde,* "that the motive for this attack was apparently a long-standing animosity between Miss Starbuck and yourself, Baron?"

Only now did the baron look at Jessie. His blue eyes settled coldly on her for a moment. "Yes, Señor," he said smoothly. "Miss Starbuck inherited her father's vast business holdings. They include many enterprises that are in direct competition with enterprises in which my associates and I are engaged. Over the years we have often seen examples of the Starbuck predilection for violence. Her father personally killed the son of a business associate of mine—and bragged about it and defied the man to do anything about it. The man did, in fact, do something about it. He caused the death of Alex Starbuck. At other times, warehouses have been burned, trains wrecked, grainfields burned, cattle stolen. Miss Starbuck has inherited all her father's traits, including a short temper and a willingness to kill her rivals in business. I am afraid, Señor, that, being a wealthy and powerful family, the Starbucks have lost the human ability to accept occasional defeats. When they are bested in a business transaction, they strike out and kill."

Jessie rose to her feet, seething with anger. "If you please, sir," she snapped at the *alcalde*, "I can prove that every word this man has spoken, of me and of my father, is a lie. It will require only a few days to assemble the evidence and bring here a score of witnesses—"

"Where are these witnesses, Miss Starbuck?" asked the *alcalde*.

She drew a breath. "In the United States, most of them," she admitted.

"Yes. So it would not be a few days. It would take weeks to bring them here. But I don't think we need to hear them. *These* witnesses"—he swung his arm toward the baron and his three friends—"testify that you attacked them and killed two of their associates. Whatever may have been your motive, the facts are clear that you did attack and kill two men. Your witnesses from the United States could not address themselves to that question. They were not here. We need not delay for weeks. We have the evidence we need."

"They lie," Jessie said weakly as she dropped back to her chair.

"Yes. You will testify you did not kill those men."

"I will testify we did so, but in self-defense," she said. "They attacked us, and we defended ourselves."

The *alcalde* nodded. "You would so testify. As would, I suppose, your Japanese servant. Maybe your Mexican employee would so testify, if we could find him. But four witnesses testify that you did—"

"And more, Señor," the baron interrupted. "Those men so badly wounded that they cannot be here today will also testify if necessary."

Don Francisco nodded. "Yes," he said. "I do not think we require much more."

Jessie heard a metallic thud and swung around to see Ki's handcuffs on the floor behind him. He sprang to his feet and, with a chop to the bridge of the nose of one, a

51

kick to the groin of the other, knocked two of the *rurale* guards sprawling. Throwing himself behind the chairs, he aimed a sideways kick at the belly of a third and sent him backward into the fourth. Both of them fell.

Captain Ortiz reached for his revolver, but Jessie had already drawn her derringer from behind her belt buckle, and she held it leveled at the captain's chest. "Drop it," she said.

The captain dropped his pistol to the carpeted floor. The baron and his men sat transfixed, staring. They had seen Ki's *shuriken* fly before, and did not want to risk seeing them again.

The *alcalde* sat calmly behind his desk. His watery old eyes lay unmoving on Jessie and Ki as they backed toward the double doors at the rear of the chamber.

The anteroom was vacant, and they hurried unimpeded into the corridor.

"How did you do that?" Jessie asked as they ran. "I swear, you still surprise even me sometimes."

"It wasn't very hard," Ki explained between breaths. "I just expanded the muscles of my wrists when they put the shackles on me. That gave me a little room to work. Then I just squeezed my knuckles together and they popped right off." He stopped Jessie with a firm hand on her arm. "I think we'd better not enter that courtyard. Up these stairs. Maybe we can reach the roof."

The upper floor of the building seemed to be abandoned, though it was the site of a number of small offices they passed as they trotted along the upstairs corridor. Ki ducked into one room after another, looking out the window of each. In one, he beckoned Jessie to join him. The window there opened on a tiled roof, and he dropped easily and waited for her as she—impeded a bit by her shackles—made an awkward exit and dropped beside him.

They were on an outside roof that sloped away to a street behind the government compound. Ki lowered Jessie by her upstretched arms and dropped her the remaining four feet. Then he jumped down.

For the moment the street was quiet, though they could

hear shouting from inside the compound as *rurales* were called out to search for the two escaped prisoners. Jessie and Ki ran along the street, conspicuous to passersby, who stared at them. It was a street of prosperous homes with blank façades and barred doors. These homes probably had pleasant gardens behind, but they presented only a solid wall to the street, with few windows. For Jessie and Ki there was no option but to get out of that street, into an intersecting street, and from there to go . . . where?

A soldier appeared ahead, having emerged from a gate in the compound wall. He shouted an alarm, and in a moment he was joined by four others. They were only twenty yards away, and they did not run after Jessie and Ki, who had reversed and begun to run for the other end of the street. They simply knelt and aimed their rifles.

Jessie looked back. Five rifles were aimed at their backs. She stopped. Ki had seen the same thing. He stopped. They raised their hands and stood waiting to be retaken.

For a moment in the courtyard, Jessie feared she and Ki were about to be shot by a firing squad. They were led to a wall, and a squad of soldiers knelt a few yards away and aimed their rifles at them. But Captain Ortiz approached them. He reached under Jessie's belt and pulled out her derringer. Then he barked angry commands at his soldiers, and a squad of ten came to take Ki away. The captain and five others led her across the courtyard and into a small guardroom, where she was ordered to sit, and two soldiers held their rifles on her.

After a few minutes, Captain Ortiz returned. He was carrying a bundle of white fabric. It was a simple cotton dress. "Now, Miss Starbuck," he said, "we will see what other concealed weapons you are carrying. Take off your clothes and put on that dress instead."

He unlocked her handcuffs. She had no choice; under his eyes and those of the two soldiers, she took off her jeans and shirt and boots and stood naked before them for a moment, until she could pick up the white dress from the floor and pull it over her head. Captain Ortiz examined her clothes carefully, looking for another derringer, or a knife, or whatever else she might be carrying. He found nothing.

"You look like a woman now, anyway," the captain said.

She did look like a woman of the village. The dress was scooped shallowly across her bosom, showing her shoulders but covering her breasts. The skirt was short, ending at mid-calf.

They led her again across the central courtyard of the government compound. Her bare feet were bruised by the loose gravel, but they marched her quickly, forcing her to keep up with them. On the far side they entered the stable and blacksmith shop, and there she saw Ki kneeling before an anvil. They were riveting chains on him. He was stripped to the simple white loincloth he wore under his trousers, and his ankles were already shackled with a short chain. The smith was pounding a hot rivet into a manacle, fastening it so tightly on Ki's wrist that there was no possibility of his squeezing out.

"And . . . I too?" she whispered.

"Of course. You and the Japanese are a dangerous pair."

They forced her to sit on a wooden bench and rest her ankles on the anvil. The muscular, barechested smith fitted shackles to her, beating them with his hammer to adjust them tightly. When he was satisfied with them, he took hot rivets from his forge, handling them with tongs, and put them through holes in the steel bands, then pounded them to spread them. The shackles would have to be cut off; they could not be removed otherwise.

They forced her to kneel then, as Ki had done, and the smith riveted manacles on her wrists.

The chains were heavy, far heavier than the other manacles had been. She knew she was helpless, well beyond making any further effort to escape or defend herself from whatever these men decided to do with her. She did not cry. But as she trudged again across the courtyard, she had never felt so bereft of hope.

Ki continued to look stoic. He kept the same unreadable expression he had shown them in the chamber of the *alcalde*, until he made his move. Even when he was chained, the soldiers moved cautiously beside him.

They stood before the *alcalde*. Their chairs had been removed. The baron and his men sat again where they had been before, their cold eyes fixed on the two prisoners.

"If there had been doubt," said the *alcalde*, "that you are as the witnesses have described you, a violent, murderous woman, you have now removed that doubt. If I entertained any reluctance to deal with you as the law requires, it is gone. I find you guilty of murder."

"We are *not* guilty," Jessie whispered hoarsely.

"What do you do with murderers in Texas, Miss Starbuck?"

Jessie drew a deep breath. "We hang them," she said softly.

"And so do we here," said the *alcalde*.

"You must inform the President of Mexico," she said weakly. "He must inform my government first."

"It is my sentence," Don Francisco said calmly, "that you be suspended by the neck and left hanging so until you are dead. May God have mercy on your souls."

They were taken, she and Ki, to the cellar beneath the building, where apparently the town of La Paz de Cristo had but one prison cell, an ironbound cage in the middle of a stone-walled room. Both of them were put in that cage, and two soldiers sat as guards near the door to the room.

The cage had a wooden bucket for slops but no furniture, and there was nowhere to sit but on the stone floor. Jessie sat disconsolately and let her forehead drop to her drawn-up knees.

"I see no way out of this, do you?" she asked Ki.

"No," he said. "None."

They had been in the cage about an hour when Baron Otto vom und zum Heligendorf came puffing down the stairs and into the room. He took one of the soldiers' chairs and sat down facing Jessie through the heavy iron grille of the cage.

"Well," he said. "I suppose you understand it all now, Miss Starbuck." He sighed. "I almost regret it. It has been a challenge to trap you. A real challenge. For a moment this afternoon I thought you had won again."

"Since I came to New Orleans, every attempt to kill me has been yours, I suppose," she said. She came to the grille, to stand and face him directly. "Twice in New Orleans—"

The baron grinned and interrupted. "And twice here. From the crude attempts in New Orleans, I discovered you were tough and shrewd and well protected—entirely capable of defending yourself. Last night I sent Heinrich with his dynamite. He had never failed before; he is a much more capable man than the two in New Orleans. He not only failed, but lost his right hand. Then this morning you fought off a whole troop of my best men."

"How clever of you to turn all that into a murder charge against us," Jessie said, her voice dripping with sarcasm.

"Oh, that was not so clever. The *alcalde* is of course in my employ. You would have been arrested today or tomorrow in any case, and he would have found you guilty of some crime, enough to justify his hanging you. It is very good for us, though."

"What you have done will be found out," she said grimly. "You will suffer for it."

The baron shrugged. He reached up to where her hand clutched a bar of the grille and touched the manacle on her wrist. "A pretty thing, this," he said. "I wish it were possible to keep you alive, in chains. I would love to take you home with me, to keep you . . . ah, well. You will be buried in them."

"At least you will have the hanging to amuse you," she said bitterly.

"I'm afraid not," he said. "My stomach won't endure the sight. In any event, duty calls. My men and I will be leaving tonight. This is farewell, Miss Starbuck. I do salute you."

They were given bread and cheese and, to their surprise, a large jug of red wine. They ate and drank little. When the sun set, the room and the cage were lighted only by a small, flickering candle on the floor between the guards. They sat on the stone floor, their backs to the guards.

"Ramondo..." said Jessie. "Is it possible he saw the attack coming and just ran away? If so, maybe he carried word of us back to Veracruz."

"No," said Ki. "I saw him in the courtyard this afternoon. The *alcalde* said they couldn't find him, but he was here."

"Then Bragg is working for the baron, too."

"Likely," said Ki.

Jessie gingerly turned the shackle around her ankle, trying to relieve a bit of the pressure on her flesh. "Oh, Ki," she whispered. "This is my fault. I should not have insisted on riding up here from Veracruz alone. It was impetuous, stupid."

"I have failed you, Jessie," said Ki sadly.

"No! How can you say that?"

"I promised your father I would protect you, would never let anything like this happen. And now—"

Jessie reached for his hand. "Ki," she said. "A woman could not have had a better friend than you have been to me. You have saved my life a hundred times. But what you have been to me is more important. All these years I have had what few people ever have—a friend in whom I could always place absolute confidence, for loyalty, for honesty, for courage—"

"You have learned courage too," said Ki.

"I hope I have it in the morning," said Jessica.

★

Chapter 6

It was, of course, impossible to sleep. Even Ki, with his practiced discipline, was restless all night. Lying on the cold stone floor in her chains, filled with dread of the morning, Jessie rolled painfully on the stones, sometimes sat up, sometimes stood. Her thoughts, much of the night, were of her parents, of how her father had been killed defending what he had built, of how her mother had died at the hands of the group here represented by the baron. Her father had anticipated his death and prepared her and trusted her to take control after him; and now, in so short a time, she was defeated and the Starbuck empire was at an end.

She had never seen a hanging. She knew, though, that everything depended on the skill of the hangman. If he knew his work, a person died quickly, probably without much pain. If he did not—or if he simply wanted to inflict pain—the hanged person slowly strangled at the end of the rope, kicking, choking, suffering protracted agony. Anyway, it was a horrible and shameful way to die.

She was afraid. She did not need to speak of it to Ki. He knew. He would go with dignity, outwardly calm. She was not sure she could. She hoped they hanged them simultaneously. She did not want to see Ki die, and she did not want him to see her lose her courage.

She saw the red light of dawn fill the tiny barred window high in the stone wall.

It was bright outside, long after dawn, when Captain Ortiz entered the room. He stepped to the grille and looked down at Jessie and Ki sitting on the floor.

"Is it now?" Jessie asked hoarsely.

"Is what now, Miss Starbuck?" the captain asked.

"Are you going to hang us now?"

Captain Ortiz shook his head. "No. Not today, Miss Starbuck. I was compelled to remind the *alcalde* this morning that I cannot, by law, conduct an execution until the warrant has been signed by the governor. I sent a messenger bearing the warrants this morning, but I am sure he will require at least a day to reach the governor and a day to return. Indeed, it is possible the governor will want to review the case and will not sign the warrants immediately." The captain smiled thinly. "No, Miss Starbuck. You will have to wait."

Jessie rose and came to the grille. "Will you, then, at least send word to Veracruz, to Monsieur Henri Derval at the Hotel Real, telling him what has happened?"

Captain Ortiz shrugged. "I suppose, in the circumstances, I should grant reasonable requests. Henri Derval, you say? A Frenchman?"

The messenger with the warrants for execution did not return the next day, or the day after, or the day after that. For four days Jessie and Ki sat miserably on the stone floor of the cage, their wrists and ankles chafing under their manacles and shackles, their muscles cramping from the restrictions on their movement. They had no reason to believe that Henri Derval, even if he was found and came, could do anything to help them; and in any case, it was just as likely that the signed warrants would come first, and Henri would arrive only to be shown their graves. The suspense added immeasurably to their wretchedness.

Then, on the evening of their fourth full day in the cage, Captain Ortiz strode dramatically into the room, bringing Henri Derval.

"Ho," said the captain grudgingly. "Your friend is a persuasive fellow. He places me in a position of great awkwardness."

"Not so awkward as being hanged, Captain, let me assure you," said Henri.

"He has almost convinced me," said the captain to Jessica, "that even if the governor signs the warrants, I should delay the execution until the matter can be brought to the attention of the President."

"What of the *alcalde?*" Jessica asked.

"He cannot hang you himself," said Captain Ortiz. "And I will not do so until all doubt has been resolved. You may regard yourself as under a reprieve. It may be temporary, I warn you. I will leave you to talk with your friend."

The captain left, and Henri reached through the iron grille to touch Jessie's cheek. "Ah, to see you so, Jessie, is most painful."

She held up her chained wrists. "Could you talk him into taking these off us?" she asked.

"One thing at a time, as you Americans are fond of saying," said Henri. "I have sent a messenger to the governor, Don Perfecto Morelos, bearing a petition on your behalf. It was countersigned by the United States consul at Veracruz, also by the French consul."

"What about the new American embassy counsellor, the ex-congressman who sailed to Veracruz with us on the *Sarah?*"

Henri's face darkened. "He refused, as he said, to involve himself in the matter." Henri glanced at Ki. "His young daughter wept when she heard the two of you were to be hanged."

"And the baron?" she asked.

"Yes, the baron," said Henri. "The baron returned to Veracruz just before I left. He went aboard the *Sarah,* with his confederates, and the *Sarah* sailed for Havana."

"He thinks Ki and I are dead, I suppose."

"I did not tell him you are not."

"Susan's father probably did," said Ki. "I mean Congressman McPherson."

"No," said Henri. "McPherson left for Mexico City shortly after refusing to help me, and he was gone by the time the baron arrived."

"The baron is a dangerous enemy," said Ki.

"Yes," said Jessie. "You must understand, Henri, that by involving yourself with us, you make a thousand enemies."

Henri Derval smiled and shrugged. "Maybe not so many as that," he said. "Most of that thousand are my enemies already, I suspect."

Captain Ortiz refused to take the chains off his prisoners. He allowed himself to be persuaded, however, to send in cots and a table and chairs, and he allowed Henri to arrange for meals to be served for them. He even let Henri enter the cage and sit down to dinner with them, to eat the best meals that could be bought in La Paz de Cristo. The captain also agreed to their being taken out into the courtyard for an hour each day, to walk in the sunlight, to exercise. Though their steps had to be short, the exercise relieved some of the cramps in their legs, and in the cage Ki showed Jessie how to exercise her arms and keep her muscles in condition. She watched him and followed him also in a form of exercise that involved pushing and pulling immovable things—the walls, the floors, even the chains themselves—which he performed to keep his muscles hard.

Three more days passed. They had been prisoners for a week, and the messenger had not returned with the warrants of execution. Jessie became more optimistic as time passed; still, she reminded herself often that the warrants could come anytime and the captain might feel compelled to hang her and Ki. He was grim when he saw them. He warned them that their execution had not been canceled, only postponed, and he did not mean to do them the cruelty of raising hopes that would have to be dashed.

* * *

On Sunday the bells rang in the morning, summoning the faithful to the churches. In the afternoon they rang again, this time differently, with a more urgent note, and at a time when there was no religious reason for them to ring. Jessie was troubled by the sound. It could mean the arrival of someone bearing word from the governor. It could announce the hanging. Shortly they heard the sound of twenty or more horsemen galloping into the courtyard, and of men shouting. There was a disturbance above, and then men came stomping down the stairs.

A man in a black sombrero, wearing a slim-cut black suit trimmed with silver thread, strode into the room. He wore an iron-gray, spade-shaped beard, and had a thin cigar clenched in his teeth. He stepped immediately to the grille of the cage. "You are Jessica Starbuck?" he asked, frowning.

She nodded. "Yes," she said quietly.

"I would have known without asking. You look like your father. I am Don Perfecto Morelos, Governor of Veracruz." He bowed curtly, then turned to the men behind him and growled angry orders in Spanish. "You will be freed from this place immediately and those chains cut off. When you have had time to bathe and dress, we will meet and discuss what is to be done."

"You knew my father?" Jessica managed to ask.

"I would be a poor man if not for the honesty and generosity of Alex Starbuck," he said.

The chains that had been put on in a few minutes required an hour of laborious sawing to remove. The blacksmith worked at it with the same disinterested, laconic air with which he had worked to put them on. He was a craftsman, and in spite of their impatience he would not strike with a hammer and chisel, even when the manacles and shackles were almost sawed through, for fear of injuring Jessie and Ki even slightly. While Jessie was led off by sympathetic women to a warm, scented bath, Ki bathed more quickly, in cold water, and set about recovering his weapons and their other property. With the cooperation of Captain Ortiz, he was able to regain everything, including their clothes and other gear, and even their horses.

By the time his work was finished and Jessie had bathed and dressed, they had in hand the written invitation of Governor Morelos to take dinner with him in the home of Don Francisco Tolosa, the *alcalde*. Jessie had carried no dresses on their trek out of Veracruz, and she wore for the evening a skirt and blouse provided by the women assigned to care for her. The voluminous blouse hung loose over her breasts, but it left her shoulders bare. The fabric was black, elaborately embroidered in designs representing large flowers in bright colors. The skirt was white, and embroidered with white thread in subtle design. The women had told her this was the native costume of the next province south—Chiapas—and had convinced her she should go barefoot as every woman wearing this costume would. Her long blond hair fell over her bare shoulders. There were wide bruises and a band of scabs from the shackles around her wrists and ankles, but her radiant beauty made it easy not to notice these signs of her recent travail.

Henri Derval was a guest, as was Captain Ortiz. The fat *alcalde* sat at the foot of his table, having surrendered the head to the governor. Jessie sat to the governor's right, Henri to his left, and Ki and the captain faced each other across the middle of the table.

"The evidence," protested the *alcalde* when the governor directed him to apologize to Jessie and Ki. "The testimony of the witnesses—"

"You're an old fool, Francisco," said the governor. "You have held office too long. As of tonight, you are retired. I have appointed Captain Ortiz the new *alcalde* of La Paz de Cristo."

The old man shrugged. "If you have heard the testimony—"

"How much did the baron pay you, Don Francisco?" Jessie asked coldly.

The old man's face burned.

"How much, Francisco?" the governor demanded.

"Uhhmm, a thousand pesos," said the old man, frowning.

"You would not have corrupted yourself for a mere thousand," said the governor. "Five thousand, I should guess. Am I right?"

"No, no. Not five. Two."

"Five," said the governor. "So tomorrow you will make a gift to the church of ten thousand pesos. Ten thousand. It will express your thanks to God that these people were not hanged—in which case I would have hanged *you.*"

Captain Ortiz, the new *alcalde,* laughed, and the tension was eased. The old man—as Ki noticed—was not so distressed that he was unable to drink thirstily and eat hungrily, and shortly he was somnolently drunk on wine.

"When I learned," said the governor a few minutes later, "that Baron Heligendorf was involved in your problem, Miss Starbuck, I was immediately alerted. I have been aware for some time of his activities in Veracruz. I am not in the least surprised to hear that you suspect he is behind the loss of your ships."

"To which of his activities do you refer, Don Perfecto?" Henri asked.

"For some time we have been aware that quantities of guns and ammunition have been entering the port of Veracruz. We became alarmed at first because we supposed someone might be arming an insurgent movement. But the arms are not leaving Veracruz by road. They go out again on ships, smaller ships, and we have not yet learned their destination. What is more, we have noticed a number of pistoleros coming into Veracruz. They, too, soon disappear, leaving the port for an unknown destination."

"Someone," said Jessie, "is assembling an invasion force and they are stealing Starbuck ships to carry that force."

"I suspect that is correct," said the governor.

"The baron is their arms dealer. He buys weapons in the United States and elsewhere and ships them to Veracruz on my ships."

"The *federales,*" said Captain Ortiz, "maintain an army post at Tampico. Three months ago it was discovered that the major commanding that post was unable to account for six small field guns and a quantity of ammunition for them. He had sold the guns, no one knows to whom. I imagine the incident is related."

"This is exactly the method of operation of Baron Heligendorf," said Henri.

"We don't know that the baron had anything to do with it," said the governor. "But . . ." He shrugged.

"A report of all this should be sent immediately to your government in Washington," said Captain Ortiz.

"I am afraid," interjected Ki quietly, "that highly placed persons in Washington already know about it."

Jessie looked at Ki curiously. "Ki," she said, "do you have concrete evidence to that effect?"

He smiled faintly. "You will recall I spent a few pleasant hours chatting with Susan McPherson, while we were passengers together aboard the *Sarah*. She spoke of conversations she had overheard between her father and the baron. Whatever the baron is involved in, her father is involved in as well. And, since he is involved, so is James G. Blaine in some way. So, too, is Secretary of State Frelinghuysen. They promised her father a diplomatic post in Paris in return for his cooperation as a member of Congress."

"Why, then, is he in Mexico?" asked Jessica.

"One must suspect it is to neutralize the governments of the United States and Mexico when the baron's group makes its move. The President of the United States will rely on the United States embassy in Mexico City for his information . . ."

"And," interrupted the governor, "the American ambassador has been called home for talks at the State Department. That leaves Congressman McPherson in charge temporarily—maybe exactly at the critical point."

"The recovery of the Starbuck ships suddenly coincides with the national interests of the United States," said Henri.

"What can we do?" asked Jessie.

"I suggest we secretly arm the next Starbuck ship that safely reaches Veracruz," said Henri. "If it is attacked, it can defend itself and maybe capture some of the pirates."

"The Bay of Snakes," said Jessie, smiling wryly.

"There are no ships there," said Captain Ortiz. "I sent a squad to look, as soon as Monsieur Derval told me you expected to find ships there."

"No, of course not," said Jessie. "Andrew Bragg sent us up the coast toward the bay to lure us into the baron's traps. Mr. Bragg has much to account for."

"I can provide guns to arm a Starbuck ship," said the governor. "Would any of your sailors know how to operate a Gatling gun?"

"I can operate a Gatling gun," said Henri.

"It would offer a nasty surprise to a pirate ship closing to grapple," said the governor. "And we can put two or three small field guns on board. You can give a Starbuck ship a fierce bite."

"I think any effort will require men," said Henri.

"Captain?" the governor inquired. "You owe Miss Starbuck a service, do you not?"

Captain Ortiz nodded gravely. "I will be please to lead a force of *rurales* to assist you," he said.

"It is settled, then," said the governor. "I will come to Veracruz to join the effort in a week or ten days. Unhappily, I have other duties that demand my attention in the meantime."

In the saddle again, riding the chestnut mare for which she had developed some affection, Jessie quickly recovered her strength and her optimism. She rode beside Henri, and Ki rode beside Captain Ortiz, at the head of a column of twenty *rurales*. They dragged the two small field guns the governor had provided, and he had promised that the Gatling gun would arrive in Veracruz in a few days.

As they rode south toward Veracruz, from time to time they had a view of the sea from atop a rise of land, and they could see sailing ships a few miles out, on the run from Tampico to Veracruz. Captain Ortiz offered Jessie his fieldglass; scanning the ships, she was able to identify one flying the Starbuck house flag. That was good. She would commandeer that ship to be armed and take part in their plan.

They camped one night near the beach, and she and Henri were able to ride a little distance from the camp and swim in the warm salt water and make love on the sand.

Early in the evening of the second day, they rode into Veracruz. The *rurales* took their field guns to the *presidio*, and Jessie, Ki, Henri, and Juan rode to the Hotel Real. It was Jessie's intention to confront Andrew Bragg immediately, and as soon as their horses and gear were taken in charge by the *hotelero*, they set out for the Starbuck offices.

There were no offices anymore. There was no Andrew Bragg. As soon as they entered the street they saw the shattered, burned wreckage of the building. Two days ago, as they learned through the *alcalde* of Veracruz, the offices of Starbuck Shipping had been destroyed by a dynamite blast. Andrew Bragg and two clerks had been killed.

"Heinrich," muttered Ki.

Jessie nodded. "The baron's bomb man. Even without his right hand..."

There was other news. A messenger from the offices of the maritime insurance underwriters waited for Jessie at the hotel when she returned. The *Sarah*, he said, had never reached Havana.

The Starbuck ship they had seen was in port. The captain, summoned to the Hotel Real, identified his ship as the *Lone Star*, a square-rigger of three hundred tons, ninety feet long — a little less than half the size of the *Sarah*. Astounded to meet his ship's owner in Veracruz, Captain Putnam assured Jessie that his ship was stout, handy, and able to do any service she might require. Jessie told him to keep quiet, even about meeting with her, but to unload his Veracruz cargo and be ready to receive her orders.

She dined that evening in the hotel with Ki, Henri, and Captain Ortiz — now resplendent in red and blue uniform and black varnished boots. As they sat and talked after their dinner, Ki touched her hand and nodded toward the door. Congressman McPherson and his wife and daughter had just entered the dining room. The congressman saw them only as he walked past their table, too near to fail to acknowledge their presence. He bowed curtly.

"I cannot express to you," Jessie said to him, "all my appreciation for the help you afforded us when we needed it."

"I was confident," said the congressman coldly, "that it was a minor matter and that you, with your own considerable resources, would deal with it handily."

"I will express my thanks in a letter to the President," said Jessie.

The congressman bowed again. "All's well that ends well, Miss Starbuck," he said, and turned and walked away.

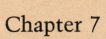

Chapter 7

The hotel was comfortable, but Ki did not sleep well in Veracruz. The tropical night sounds, a constant chittering of tiny creatures in the garden and the trees, underlying the muffled roar of all-night revelry in the street, obscured any tiny noises that might serve to warn him of danger to himself or Jessie.

It was after midnight. The sounds of laughter from Jessie's room, which she was sharing with Henri Derval, had ceased half an hour ago. Ki was dozing lightly. Suddenly his eyes opened, the transition from sleep to wakefulness so instantaneous that it was as though he had not slept at all. He had heard a sound. But not a sound. At least it was not something he had heard with his ears, but with a sense that was beyond the physical senses, the warrior's faculty called *zanshin*, or "lingering awareness." It told him of the presence of someone outside his door.

Slipping out of bed, he took up a position next to the armoire on the opposite side of the room from the door, from where, in the deepest shadow in the room, he could see anyone who entered.

He did not sleep with his door locked. Having to unlock the door would impede him, perhaps fatally, if he had to rush to Jessie's room. In any case, it had become a habit with him to memorize the sound made by an opening door in any place where he might be sleeping; even the softest, most careful turning of a doorknob would not fail to wake him.

The knob turned. He watched the door swing silently inward. The dim light of the hall filled his room. Then the shadow of someone coming in blocked that light for a moment. The shadow passed quickly through the door and shut it.

"Ki?"

"Susan?"

"Oh, Ki!"

She groped at the bed for a moment, then turned toward the shadow from which she had heard the sound of his voice. She did not see him but came to him anyway, because that shadow was the only place where he could be.

She gasped as her hands found him. He was naked. For an instant she hesitated, and then she threw her arms around him and clasped herself to him and kissed him.

"I was afraid," she said. "I was so unhappy! They told us the Mexicans had hanged you and Miss Starbuck."

He held her in his arms. Her hair and face had the clean, fresh smell of perfumed soap. He could tell what she was wearing—a nightgown and a robe.

"When I saw you in the dining room, I was too stunned to speak," she whispered. "They hadn't told me you were not hanged."

"Who?" he asked. "Who told you we were?"

"A man who came to Mexico City. He had a German accent, so heavy you could hardly understand him. He told my father you and Miss Starbuck had been hanged, at the town of La Paz de Cristo. Oh, Ki! My father was glad to hear it!" She sobbed. "Why, Ki? Why would my father want to see you dead?"

"That's a long story," said Ki. He stroked her hair. "Susan, you . . . you woke me. I am not clothed."

"I know," she whispered. She ran her hands over his bare back, then down and over his naked buttocks. She kissed his throat. "I know!"

His member had stiffened, and now it rose. She could not help but feel it swell between them, pressing against her lower belly. She did feel it. She shoved her hand between his body and hers, and touched it.

"Susan," he said. "Susan, no. You are a girl, a virgin, I suppose. I can't—"

"I am eighteen years old," she said. "I am a virgin, yes— in body, but certainly not in spirit. I want you to make me a woman, Ki. I want it from *you!*"

He nuzzled her neck. "It wouldn't be right," he whispered in her ear. "Someday you will marry."

"Oh, yes," she sneered. "Maybe to Reinhard Heligendorf, the baron's son. My father has talked about the possibility. Why do I have to wait for some German pig to do for me what I want you to do now? It's a very intimate thing, Ki. Don't I have the right to choose who does it?"

"Women rarely have that choice, it seems," he said.

"But why not?"

He could see her face, colorless in the nearly nonexistent light of the hotel room, could see her turned-up little nose, her rosebud mouth, her full round cheeks. He could feel her soft breasts pressed against him.

"Please, Ki," she whispered.

He nodded, then lifted her in his arms and carried her to his bed. On the way she began to pull off her clothes, and when he put her down she finished and threw them aside. He closed the shutters over the window, latched the door, and struck a lucifer to light the bedside lamp. The yellow lamplight gleamed on her plump little body. Her skin was pale. Her breasts were surprisingly full for a girl her age. Her little belly was round and full, too. Her eyes glistened brightly in the yellow glow of the lamp.

For a while they sat together on the bed, with their backs against the headboard, while Susan acquainted herself intimately with all his male parts. She felt his shaft, pulling it upward, squeezing gently to feel its hardness. She pressed

73

his legs apart and ran her fingertips over the pendulous skin bag beneath his member. She lifted her breasts in her own hands and offered them to him to caress and squeeze. When he bent down and sucked her nipples into his mouth, she moaned and arched her body.

He slipped a finger into the warm, wet valley between her legs, and while she gasped and writhed, he explored and found she was indeed a virgin; her maidenhead was intact. He decided he should take her in the missionary position, which would give him complete control over his penetration and let him make it gentle and no deeper than she could accept.

When he rolled her over and rose above her, he asked her if she was sure she really wanted this.

"More than anything in the world," she whispered.

For a few minutes he toyed with their parts, rubbing himself against her slit, covering his shaft with her copious lubrication. She seemed to think this was what it amounted to, and shortly he had to quiet her, to settle her in position. Then, placing himself, he entered her—only a little at first, just to the point where her hymen would have to yield to his first real thrust.

"Oh!" she cried, her blue eyes widening.

"There is more, Susan," he said to her gently. "We don't have to do more."

"Give me a moment," she murmured.

He nodded and waited, caressing her cheek with his hand.

Susan's eyes were fixed on his face. Her cheeks were bright red. She drew a deep breath. "Now," she said suddenly.

He thrust. The hymen stretched and broke, and his shaft plunged deep into her. She moaned with hurt and pleasure at the same time. He waited for a moment. She did not wait. To his surprise, she began to arch and fall back, arch and fall back again, making thrusts for him. He matched her rhythm and thrust to meet her when she arched. Immediately he was driving as far into her as this position would allow. She pulled her legs from under him and locked one ankle over another behind his thighs, accommodating deeper penetration. Her face gleamed red, she squeezed her eyes tight shut and sucked and blew deep breaths, one after another.

In a short time she stiffened in her orgasm, and at that moment he let himself have his. They weakened together, their strength flowing into their loins and dissipating in their overpowering passion. He rolled off her, keeping her body clasped to his and his shaft in her, and they lay, sweating, breathing hard, relaxing. She whispered to him that she was grateful.

Susan remained with him two hours more. He was her teacher, she said, and she wanted to learn more.

She told him, as they lay together, that her father had returned to Veracruz at the summons of the baron. Her father had been disappointed, she said, that the baron was not here.

"But the baron sailed for Havana the day after he returned here from La Paz de Cristo," said Ki.

"My father expected the baron to be in Veracruz," said Susan. "No one said anything about Havana."

Ki kept his next thought to himself—that the *Sarah,* in which the baron had sailed for Havana, had never reached there. Maybe the baron had known it wouldn't. Undoubtedly he had known it wouldn't. He and his assassins had seized the *Sarah* shortly after it left Veracruz. It must be somewhere nearby, then, the biggest ship the cartel had stolen, about to become the flagship of a pirate fleet.

It was difficult to focus on the fate of ships with Susan urging him to show her more. He taught her the eroticism of her own body, things she had suspected but of which, in her girlish innocence, she had only a little imperfect knowledge. He showed her how to use her own fingers when she was alone, to induce the most delicious sensations for herself. After she had brought herself to an orgasm as he showed her, he put his tongue to her small bud and quickly brought her to a different, more intense climax. A little later he taught her to kneel on the bed and present herself to him for entry from the rear. She was reluctant to

75

do that, at first, but when she felt the pleasure it brought, she moaned and urged him to thrust into her even more deeply.

"Ki," she said when finally she was exhausted and lay quietly on her back. "I think I've been very lucky. I've been initiated by a master. Did you teach Miss Starbuck the same things?"

He shook his head firmly. "No, Susan," he said.

She smiled. "You're a gentleman. You won't talk about me, either."

"Jessie," he said thoughtfully, "is a beautiful woman, a desirable woman in every way. We are friends, Jessie and I—friends and more. But I have never touched her, never will, never can."

Before dawn, he checked the hall for Susan as he had checked the passageway between the cabins on the ship, and with a final kiss she slipped out and hurried toward the stairs to the next floor and to her own room.

The Gatling gun promised by Governor Morelos arrived the next night and was hauled under cover of darkness into a stable in the *presidio*. Henri Derval examined it and, with enthusiasm, pronounced it in good condition and suitable for his plans. Captain Abel Putnam of the *Lone Star* spent hours with Jessie, learning how the Starbuck ships had been taken, how they were undoubtedly being made a part of a pirate fleet being readied for some sort of filibustering expedition against one nearby small nation or another, and how Jessie wanted him to use his ship, the *Lone Star*, as an armed decoy.

Captain Putnam was an old sea dog who had once been master of a whaler, and he took to his role with animated vigor. Aboard the *Lone Star* in the harbor, Jessie had difficulty restraining him, keeping him quiet about their plans until the ship was well out to sea. The Gatling gun and the two small field guns that were to be mounted on the ship's deck were important secrets that must not be leaked to anyone in the port. They were brought to the dock in the middle of the night, in two covered wagons, and were hauled aboard and stowed under tarpaulins. The crew of the ship was told that the tarps covered a steam engine and pumps for pumping the water out of a mine in Honduras.

The *Lone Star*'s passenger accommodations were cramped and primitive. Even so, she carried two passengers bound for Colón, in Panama. Captain Putnam told them his ship would have to lay up for repairs in Veracruz for at least two weeks and that he had found them cabins on another ship for Colón. The two grudgingly left the ship—two surly Americans with guns strapped to their hips.

Ki had begun to wonder if the Starbuck ships were actually being seized by other ships, or if they were being captured by traitors among their crew and gunmen among their passengers. Maybe it was both: an attack by another ship, with surrender forced by a mutiny on board. He spent a day aboard the *Lone Star* in harbor, searching the ship for hidden arms, scrutinizing the crew. He satisfied himself, as well as a man could be satisfied of such things, that the crew of this ship was made up of ordinary New England sailors, men who had served for years under the eccentric old Captain Putnam and would follow his orders without thought. So thick were their Down East accents that Ki, accustomed as he was to American speech, could hardly understand them.

Henri Derval would sail aboard the *Lone Star,* to operate the Gatling gun. With him would go ten of Ortiz's *rurales,* as riflemen and as crew for the field guns. Captain Ortiz told the sergeant in charge of these men that they would take their orders from Monsieur Derval. Once the ship was at sea and there was no chance of the secret being broadcast in the port, Captain Putnam would tell his men what they were doing and would issue guns to as many as volunteered to carry them.

Jessie, Ki, and the captain, at the head of another fifteen *rurales,* would ride southward along the coast. The *Lone Star* was to keep in sight of land, and a set of signals was arranged that would make it possible for the ship to exchange simple communications with the land party.

Captain Ortiz came to the ship in simple white civilian

clothes, to conceal his rank as a captain of *rurales*. His soldiers came aboard one or two at a time. He saw them installed in bunks and their weapons stowed, and in early evening he and Ki left the ship to return to the hotel. Ki had forgiven him for what happened at La Paz de Cristo and had even developed a measure of admiration for the man. Jessie and Henri had gone on to the hotel ahead of them, and as they walked toward the hotel, Ortiz suggested they stop in a waterfront cantina for a pot of wine or a tot of the white, angry-tasting tequila favored by the locals.

They entered the cantina. It was a saloon like saloons everywhere—offering hard liquor, but a heavy red wine instead of the beer they would have found in a Texas saloon. There were also gambling tables and the usual class of women to be found in such places. Ortiz asked for tequila for himself and Scotch whiskey for his friend. The bar had no Scotch, so Ki accepted a clay pot of wine. Ortiz drank three quick shots of the white liquor.

"Do you see a woman that appeals to you?" Ortiz asked, nodding toward the half-dozen whores clustered at the far end of the bar, limited apparently by the rules of the place from approaching and soliciting.

Ki glanced at them. "Not particularly," he said.

Ortiz grinned. The rules did not inhibit the women from tossing their heads in come-hither glances, signaling with low whistles, drawing down their blouses to show their breasts for a moment, or hoisting their skirts to show their legs.

"I'll pay if you want one," said Ortiz.

"Thank you, but I don't care for one," Ki replied.

Ortiz shook his head as he gestured toward a little girl among the older whores. "I doubt she's more than thirteen," he said. "Her parents probably sold her into prostitution."

The girl was pitiful. She was an Indian, barefoot and wearing pigtails. She saw them looking at her, and she smiled at them timidly and raised her skirt to show them she had hardly any pubic hair. Ki's heart went out to her. He remembered only too well what it was like to be a penniless, outcast child. He reached into a pocket and took out a U.S. ten-dollar goldpiece, intending to give it to the little girl.

Ortiz restrained him with a hand on his shoulder. "Your gesture will be misunderstood, my friend," the *rurale* officer said; apparently he had detected the look of sorrow in Ki's eyes. "And how long do you think it will be before those other *putas* rob her, and possibly beat her up as well?"

Ki nodded, realizing that his largesse would probably cause more harm than good.

Ortiz smiled. "You have a good heart," he said. "That pleases me."

Ki took a sip from his glass and grimaced. "Let's go," he said. "This wine has turned sour."

Ortiz paid for their drinks, and they left the cantina. Ki noticed that the little Indian girl was not among the whores anymore, and he wondered if she had been taken by a customer. The two men pushed through the jostling mob of sailors, whores, pimps, teamsters, peddlers, and thieves that thronged the street.

An anguished scream from behind them spun them both around. Two figures came running through the crowd, which was parting to make way. The first was the little Indian girl; running after her was a swarthy, big-bellied man, yelling, *"Puta! Alto, puta!"*

The girl ran past Ki and Ortiz, her terrified eyes seeing neither them nor where she was going. The man ran past, his face distorted with rage. Fifty yards farther along the street, he caught her. He grabbed her by her hair and jerked her off her feet. The girl screamed and he dropped her to the ground. The man kicked her. She screamed weakly, whimpering, choking. He kicked her again, then again.

A low *whuuup!* split the air, and suddenly the man staggered back, frantically grabbing at the lead-weighted ends of the cord that had whipped tight around his throat, shutting off his breath, strangling him. The little girl scrambled to her feet and ran again, while the man fell to his knees and struggled to unwind the cord and regain his breath. By the time he succeeded, the little girl had disappeared. He tossed down the weighted cord and, clutching his bruised throat,

79

staggered back the way he had come.

The street crowd had taken notice only for a moment. Ki walked over unnoticed and recovered his *surushin*.

"My judgment," said Ortiz wryly, "was correct when I took your clothes and chained you. You are dangerous."

Ki rewound the *surushin* around his waist, where it appeared to be only a rope belt. "Will you," he asked, "accompany me into the church in the next street?"

Ortiz nodded. "Do you want to pray?"

Inside the cavernous sanctuary, in the dim red light of candles burning in red globes, Ortiz spoke Spanish to the priest and asked, as Ki had directed him to do, for a Jesuit named Father Roberto. They sat down and waited, and in a few minutes the tall, black-bearded young priest appeared.

"I remember you," said Father Roberto in English. "The procurer you kicked in the knee will be a beggar. He is crippled."

"At the cantina called Fonda del Topo there is a small Indian girl, a prostitute no more than thirteen years old. Would a hundred American gold dollars be enough to place her in an orphanage, a school?"

"More than enough," said the Jesuit.

Ki took ten gold eagles from his pocket and handed them to Father Roberto. "Please try to find her tonight," he said. "She is hurt. Bruised. Not seriously, I think."

"Your interest?"

"The man who hurt her is not crippled. Just . . . sick for a while," said Ki. "I would hope you can find her before he recovers."

The Jesuit nodded. "I will find her," he said with certainty.

Chapter 8

Jessie and Henri sat long over their brandy and coffee in the dining room of the hotel. In the morning they would be separated again. Ki and Captain Ortiz ate at a separate table, out of respect for Jessie and Henri's wish to be alone together. The couple had a pleasant dinner and were about to go upstairs when Congressman McPherson stopped at their table.

"I wish to speak to you, Miss Starbuck, about your manservant," the Congressman said coldly.

"I have no manservant," said Jessie.

"Whatever you wish to call the Japanese," said McPherson. "I require you to keep him away from my daughter. If he casts another lustful look on her, I shall horsewhip him."

"I wouldn't try it, Mr. McPherson," said Jessie.

"Indeed? Why not?"

"Ki is entirely capable of killing you," she said, looking away from him, picking up her glass, and sipping from it.

McPherson sneered. "I really doubt it," he said.

"And of killing the assassins with whom you are associated," she said. "I suggest you don't send them to do your work."

"Killing seems to be your forte, Miss Starbuck," said McPherson. "You and your manservant—or whatever he is to you—escaped the gallows once recently. But you may not always be able to bribe your way out."

Henri stood. He seized McPherson's nose between the index and middle fingers of his right fist, clamping it tightly, painfully in a strong grip. "If ever again in my presence, you filthy cur," he growled, "you insult Miss Starbuck, you will answer to me for it. Consider this a taste of what will be in store for you." So saying, he twisted McPherson's nose until the cartilage cracked loudly and blood flowed.

The ex-congressman fled from the dining room, grabbing a napkin from a table to stanch the flow of blood from his nose.

At dawn, in the only cool hour of the day, Jessie bade Henri farewell at the steps of the hotel. She swung into the saddle of the chestnut mare, glad to be moving again, glad especially to be going on horseback out into the countryside, where she felt stronger, more effective, than she did exchanging words in an office or a hotel dining room. She glanced at Ki and felt that he entertained the same feelings.

She was wearing her jeans again, her Colt hung on her hip, and she was almost elated. Ki sat his horse easily, confidently, wearing the tattered jeans he loved, with his collarless white muslin shirt and leather vest with its many hidden weapons. Ortiz had come down from his room, dressed in the informal uniform of the *rurales*—white trousers and shirt, white hat, a cartridge belt loaded heavily with .44 cartridges. Their fifteen *rurales* from the *presidio* waited a few yards away, all armed with rifles and pistols, and wearing sombreros and crossed bandoliers over their white shirts.

Henri saluted one last time and strode off down the street, toward the dock and the ship. Jessie nodded at Ortiz, he spoke a command to his soldiers, and they swung around and rode away from the hotel.

They turned left, around the corner of the hotel, into a street leading southward. Before they had ridden twenty yards, a girl stepped out of the shrubbery beside the hotel, her blue dress spotted with dew, and stood in their way. It was Susan McPherson.

"Ki! Miss Starbuck! Please!"

Ki trotted forward. "Susan," he said. "What are you doing?"

"Ki, you must take me with you," she gasped. She looked up at Jessie. "Miss Starbuck. My father wants to kill you. He is a conspirator with your enemies. He is an evil man, and I hate him. He hurt me last night," she said, rubbing a dark bruise along the side of her face. "I can't go on living as the daughter of a man who wants to kill people like you and is this very moment sitting with men who are planning to do it. You must take me with you."

Ki looked at Jessie. "We must take her," he said solemnly.

Jessie studied his face for a moment. "As you wish, Ki," she said. "I suppose you have some responsibility."

Ki nodded.

"We'll need a horse," said Jessie.

Ortiz spoke in Spanish to one of his soldiers, who immediately dismounted and led his horse forward. "He will run to the *presidio,* requisition a horse for himself, and catch up with us," Juan explained.

"Can you mount a horse in that dress?" Jessie asked Susan.

"I can ride, Miss Starbuck," said Susan firmly. "You won't be held up by me." With quick, efficient motions she pulled off her blue silk dress and tossed it over the neck of the horse the soldier held for her. She was wearing a cambric corset cover and full-legged ladies' drawers, both of them white and trimmed with fine white embroidery and lace. With a defiant glance at Jessie, she lifted a foot to the stirrup and swung herself up into the saddle. "We should move," she said. "If they discover I've come with you, they will be firing at us from the hotel windows."

Jessie nodded and urged her mare into a trot. The little troop trotted southward through an alley of palm trees, away from the Hotel Real and toward the southern outskirts of Veracruz.

Ki rode beside Susan. Jessie rode with Ortiz. In a quarter of an hour they were at the southern limit of the port town and entering another of those Mexican roads that were nothing more than dusty or muddy tracks, when they were that. In half an hour Jessie understood that the countryside south of Veracruz was much like that to the north, except that shortly they came to a small river and had to ford the gravel riverbed, after which they saw on their right a little freshwater lake, fed by streams. The soldier who had gone for another horse soon caught up with them, and they pressed on.

Jessie was concerned that that band might interfere with the sailing of the *Lone Star*, and in midmorning they formed a defensive camp on high ground overlooking the Bahía de Campeche and settled to wait for the appearance of the ship, which had been scheduled to sail at dawn, as soon as Henri Derval boarded. They waited for two hours, scanning the waters with their fieldglasses.

In that time Jessie let Susan have a pair of her jeans, and Ki added one of his white shirts. The girl cast off her corset cover and drawers and dressed something like Jessie. To everyone's surprise, she asked for a pistol, and when a .44 revolver was handed her and she was challenged to prove she could fire it, she managed, on the fourth shot, to knock a hunk of driftwood off a stump. She had earned the right to wear the .44, Jessie declared, and Susan proudly strapped the cartridge belt around her hips and slung the pistol in its holster low on her thigh. A soldier, noting the flush the sun had already brought to her face, found a sombrero for her.

Before noon they spotted the *Lone Star* making its southward way along the coast, some fifteen miles out. As had been arranged, they fired a rocket. The little paper missile trailed an astonishing amount of white smoke as it flew up from their camp, and as they watched the ship a similar trail soon rose from its deck. Contact was established.

They rode on. The coastline turned, and their course became more westerly. The road disappeared entirely, and much of the time they were riding directly along the beach, at the edge of the surf that pounded incessantly on the sand. The *Lone Star* remained always in sight offshore, its white sails shining against the blue sky on the horizon. As the afternoon wore on, they rode along a spit of land, with salt water to both sides. To their right the inlet off the sea widened until it was miles across. They came, as Jessie had supposed they must, to where this inlet joined the sea—a connection a hundred yards wide, with a boiling tide now running through, making the ford impassable. The ford was at the edge of the village of Alvarado, and Juan said they could rest there and eat, until the tide was low and they could easily cross the ford and ride on south.

The village was tiny, occupied by a few fishermen. The priest at the little church welcomed them, though he could not hold back a disapproving comment on Jessie's and Susan's clothes.

Her father, Susan told Jessie, had been a Republican congressman from Ohio, from Cincinnati, which was her home. He had bought his seat in Congress, she said—which was possible in those days in Ohio politics. Rather, she amended her statement, it had been bought for him by the German businessmen who dominated his district. Cincinnati, she said, was a German town; its people spoke German on the streets, read a German-language newspaper, and drank beer from steins, by the gallon. German companies— meaning *German* German companies, not Cincinnati German companies—owned her father. He had helped them win favors and concessions all the years he was in Washington.

Her father, she went on, had thrown himself energetically into the Blaine presidential campaign. Thank God they lost, she added dryly. She laughed bitterly and recited the couplet

85

that had been recited even in Texas during the presidential campaign of 1876:

> *Blaine, Blaine, James G. Blaine,*
> *Continental liar from the state of Maine.*

"Sugar," Ki mused. "They want to monopolize the world's market in sugar. Remember, Susan? You told me they plan to corner the world market in sugar."

"Cuba," said Jessie suddenly. "That's what they want to do—invade Cuba. They steal Starbuck ships and use them to carry a force of hoodlums to Cuba, to overthrow the Spanish colonial government and seize the sugar plantations."

"The Spanish in Cuba," said Ortiz, "are weak. Many Cubans want liberty and would join a liberating force."

"They won't get liberation from the cartel," said Jessie. "A puppet government set up to exploit the country for the cartel's profit would enslave the population."

"The government of the United States should oppose them," said Susan. "But it won't. My father and Mr. Blaine and others have worked on that for years."

"Why is your father in Mexico, though?" Jessie asked.

"He is second-in-command, under the baron."

Ortiz frowned hard. "We are few," he said, "to oppose so big a scheme."

"If you are afraid," said Jessie, "then we may be still fewer."

Ortiz tossed his head. "I will stand beside you, Jessie," he said. "From what I've seen of you, I think you would win your fight without me, but I will stand beside you."

They forded the connection between the inlet and the sea as soon as the tide was low. Beyond, the coastline ran almost due west, and they followed the beach, with the *Lone Star* well behind them, tacking in a contrary wind. They rode hard for three hours, putting themselves as far ahead of the ship as possible, knowing it would continue all night while they had to camp. When they stopped for the night, they fired another rocket and saw another reply fired from the ship. Captain Putnam would maneuver offshore all night, so he would not outdistance them.

They camped above the beach, the fifteen soldiers in one camp, the rest of them in another a few yards away. Susan was disappointed to learn that Ki would not sleep beside her on the sandy ground. When they had eaten, he slipped away and began to explore the perimeter of their camp, on foot, in the dark.

He settled himself, after he had worked all the way around, in the center of a small grove of palm trees. All day he had kept watch behind, unable to believe someone was not following from Veracruz. Now he watched both ways, for anyone who might have followed them all day and for anyone who might come out from the camp to meet someone who was following.

It was past midnight when he heard the snort of a horse. He had relaxed a little, resting, and now he concentrated his senses and searched the darkness, looking for movement, listening for another sound.

His concentration was wasted. The four horsemen approached carelessly, as if they cared nothing for being heard. They rode to within a few yards of the small, thin grove where he had pressed himself against a palm and watched from the depths of a shadow so dark that he was completely immersed in it. They knew where Jessie and her party were camped. They knew and did not have to be cautious while still this far away.

So they assumed.

At the same time Ki heard the slight sound of someone behind him, approaching on foot, quietly. The traitor. He was not surprised. There was bound to be one.

The four horsemen hobbled their horses and began to move quietly toward him, toward the camp—which was two hundred yards or so behind him.

"Bitte, warten Sie eine Minute!" growled one of the men.

Ki could see them now. While the others stood impatiently and waited, the one who had spoken stepped apart from them and urinated.

They came closer. He could barely make out their outlines in the darkness of the moonless night, but three of them moved with the abrupt, crisp motions of trained soldiers, and the fourth walked more hesitantly and a little apart from the other three. They carried a load of equipment of some sort. It was too dark to see what it was.

They passed by him a few yards away, and he slipped away from the grove and followed. He followed for some distance, aware of the four but careful of the one he had heard coming out from the camp, who was now lost to him.

They moved stealthily, stopping often to listen and to peer around them, until they topped a small rise and came in sight of the camp—the two camps, actually, the *rurales* in one, Jessie and Susan and Juan Ortiz in another, smaller camp a few yards away. The camps, unfortunately, were not difficult to see. The embers of two fires glowed at their centers. The four men stood for a moment studying the camps, and then began with practiced efficiency to unpack and assemble their equipment.

Ki slipped as close as he dared, crawling on his belly. Even close up, it was difficult to see what they were doing. They pounded some kind of stakes in the ground, using muffled mauls. Then they began to attach a mechanism to those stakes. In another minute or so it was clear—they were assembling a catapult. Three men worked to assemble it. The fourth stood aside, laboriously unpacking other items. Bombs. They were putting together a catapult capable of throwing dynamite bombs into the camp. The man unpacking the bombs was working with his left hand only. It was Heinrich, the man who had lost his right hand to Ki's cleaver arrow.

Ki rose to his knees. He reached into his vest for a *shuriken*. And at that moment he felt hard steel against the back of his head.

"Careful, you yellow mongrel," growled the man behind him.

There had been five of them all along. Of course. There had to be five; otherwise how would these four have known where the camp was and where to set up their catapult? One had followed all day and had watched them establish their camp. Ki cursed his lapse of judgment.

He obeyed the man behind him and rose slowly.

"Ah," said Heinrich when he recognized him. "I only wish I had the luxury to do to you what you did to me. Unfortunately I do not. I will take a little satisfaction, though, from putting a bullet through your head. We will defer even that pleasure for a minute or two yet. I don't want to alarm your friends by firing a shot."

Ki decided he would force them to give that alarm before they could launch one of their bombs. But for a moment he would wait, examine, judge.

The catapult was like an oversized crossbow, made of steel, with a pair of cranks that pulled back on the twisted-wire bowstring. The dynamite bombs were thick arrows, with sticks of dynamite wired in a cluster around them.

"You see?" said Heinrich. "It's a very clever little apparatus. By setting the tension precisely—and knowing the weight of what we will throw—we can hurl our bombs exactly where we want them. Dieter there is quite expert. He can consistently hit a beer keg from this distance. Your people will hear the thud when the arrow arrives, and before they can decide what it is, the explosion of four sticks of dynamite will end their lives. If I had brought a small howitzer, it would hardly have been as effective."

As he spoke, Heinrich laid out four of the arrow bombs, each with a fuse sticking up from it.

"You will kill Susan McPherson," said Ki.

Heinrich shot him a hard glance. Then he shrugged.

"Does her father know she is with us?"

"Ask him," said Heinrich.

The man holding the pistol barrel to Ki's head was the ex-congressman. "You dirtied her," he muttered. "She came back to her room with the stink of you on her. She's ruined. What's more, she's run off after you and joined the Starbuck bitch, and I suppose she's been telling everything she's overheard for years." McPherson drew a breath. "So, when I see the explosion, I'm going to blow your head off. That will make me feel a little better."

The man called Dieter stood behind the catapult. He grabbed the two crank handles and turned them to draw back the wire bowstring, leaning down over the apparatus, being careful to draw the twisted wire exactly to some sort of mark scored in the steel plate of the base. Heinrich picked up a bomb and inserted it in the apparatus so that the bow-string lay in the notch at the back of the arrow around which the dynamite sticks were wrapped.

Ki composed himself. He would deal a backward kick to McPherson, then throw himself forward if he could to upset the catapult. He would shout. He doubted he could avoid McPherson's shot, but if he avoided that he would fall to a shot from one of the others. What was important was that the shot that killed him would alarm the camp. If he could knock the catapult askew, they would need time to reset it, and in that time Jessie and Ortiz could scatter and maybe even attack. He composed himself. He would try to move so that he had a chance to live, but he accepted his karma. He was calm.

Heinrich struck a wooden match. He reached toward the fuse on the bomb. But he did not light it. Instead he jerked backward as his forehead exploded with the impact of a bullet, and he fell. He was falling before Ki heard the crack of the rifle.

McPherson jumped away from Ki just as he struck backward, and the force of Ki's blow, with his elbow and heel, was dissipated. Ki swung around to find McPherson leveling his revolver at him. Then one side of McPherson's face disappeared, and he spun around and dropped. This time Ki heard the snap of a Winchester's lever action.

One of the three Germans who remained had snatched the dynamite arrow-bomb off the catapult. He had lighted a match and touched the fuse before a shot to the gut dropped him. He fell over the bomb. Ki leaped away, throwing himself in the direction from which the shots had come, which he knew now had been fired by Jessie. He found her, threw himself over her, and pinned her to the ground.

In the flash of white light from the explosion, he was lifted and tossed, with Jessie in his arms. In a cascade of sand and rocks and debris, they were thrown twenty feet from where she had crouched with her Winchester. The air was sucked from their lungs, and their bodies seemed to be afire inside and out. Landing, tumbling, they were separated and lay apart.

He struggled to lift himself to his hands and knees. Dazed and deafened, he crawled toward Jessie's inert form. "Jessie!" he yelled, and he could not hear his own voice. He rose to his knees beside her, lifting her head in his hands. "Jessie!"

Time was confused, and suddenly Ortiz was there, on his knees too, kneeling over Jessie. Then Susan dropped down beside him. Their mouths moved, but he could not hear their words. The *rurales* ran past them, toward the smoldering crater where the dynamite had exploded. The world spun around his head, and Ki fell back and lost consciousness.

★

Chapter 9

Jessie regained consciousness as she was carried back to the camp. She would have drifted away again, but in her first moment she saw two lights, red and green, hanging over the Gulf of Mexico, ten or twenty miles out. It was a signal from Henri, the signal that meant *Are you all right?* Aboard the *Lone Star* they had seen the explosion and probably heard it, and they were signaling for assurance that the landside party was still there, still functioning.

"Green rocket," she mumbled. Then again, more urgently, "Green rocket!"

Someone ran ahead, probably Ortiz. In a minute she heard the *whoosh* of the rocket, and a moment later the green flare burst above them.

In the green light she could see them carrying Ki. Susan walked beside the two *rurales* who had him. Ki looked limp.

For herself, she was aware now that part of her clothes were gone; her blouse had been shredded by the blast, and only parts of the sleeves hung around her. Her head ached. Her ears rang. Her body felt like one great bruise. She was miserable, but when she saw Ki raise his head and look up for a moment at the green flare, she felt better.

The *rurales* put them down on blankets that had been spread out for them. Ki was close to her.

"Jessie . . ." he murmured.

"Not bad shooting, huh?" she asked him weakly. "For a girl."

At dawn, Jessie and Ki went into the water. The tumbling, roaring surf refreshed them. She felt her nausea go away as the cool water swirled around her where she sat nude on the sand. Ki swam. He was marked with cuts and bruises where flying bits of debris had struck him. He had protected her from most of that.

Susan came down from the camp. She stripped and stepped into the surf. It was apparent she could not swim, but she waded out to where Ki was riding the crest of a wave toward the beach, and she was waiting for him when it tumbled him to the sand. They came back together, Ki and Susan, and sat down by Jessie.

They sat silent for a time, then Susan, staring out to sea, said quietly, "One of those men was my father. I recognized his clothes."

Ki glanced at Jessie. "We ran just before the bomb exploded," he said to Susan. "He didn't."

Susan nodded. "He came to kill us. All of us."

"You warned us," said Jessie.

"Yes."

Mountains rose just beyond the coastline where they rode that day. For Jessie and Ki it was painful to ride, but they kept an urgent pace and did not let the ship out of sight. Susan, as she had promised, did not delay them. She rode beside Ki and did not complain, though by afternoon it was apparent that she was as sore as Ki and Jessie.

In midafternoon they spotted another ship. It was a schooner, a two-master, coming from the south and west and a little closer to shore than the *Lone Star*. As they watched it through their glasses, the schooner altered course and made toward the *Lone Star*. It was a faster ship, and in the space of an hour it had closed most of the distance between itself and the *Lone Star*. They began to suspect the schooner. Its course, directly toward the *Lone Star*, had no apparent purpose—unless it was the pirate vessel, on the attack.

The party watched helplessly from the beach. They understood nothing of the sailing maneuvers, but it was plain that the schooner was heading for an encounter with the *Lone Star*. Through their telescopes they could see the crew on the deck of the schooner, men conspicuously armed, and they could see that the schooner carried naval guns, small cannon on its deck.

"I hope your friend Monsieur Derval truly understands the operation of the Gatling gun," said Ortiz after studying the schooner for some time through his long glass. "Without it, the *Lone Star* is outgunned."

On the deck of the *Lone Star*, the big green tarpaulins still covered the Gatling gun and the two small field guns. The crew went about its business, showing no sign that it was prepared for attack.

Suddenly a puff of smoke burst from the deck of the schooner. It had fired a shot from one of its guns. Sailors in the rigging of the *Lone Star* began shortening sail. Captain Putnam was slowing his ship, apparently surrendering to the pirate schooner.

Eventually the schooner turned parallel to the *Lone Star* and began to edge in, narrowing the distance between the two ships. The boarding maneuver was under way, and it was easy to imagine that it was the same kind of maneuver that had been used to capture all the other Starbuck ships.

Jessie sat astride her mare, her brass telescope to her eye. Ki stood beside her on the sand, watching without a telescope. Ortiz offered his glass to Ki from time to time, but usually Ki waved it off.

The two ships closed now, and were so close together it was difficult to distinguish all their rigging at this distance. The decks of the big ship were higher than those of the schooner, and she could see the tarpaulins still in place over the guns on the *Lone Star*. She began to wonder if Henri was really in control. Could he be a prisoner, unable to carry out his plan?

Then, as she watched, sailors ran along the front of the tarpaulins, tearing them off. She could not distinguish the Gatling gun, but in a moment she saw a staccato burst of yellow flashes, like the flashes from a string of firecrackers exploding, and the deck of the *Lone Star* was obscured in smoke. The sound came then, like the sound of twenty rifles firing in mechanical order.

Chaos erupted on the deck of the schooner. Some men ran, some fell, and she saw some jump overboard. The fire from the Gatling gun was sweeping the deck, and every man on the schooner who had not been hit was running for shelter. She saw a larger flash, then another. The *rurales* aboard the *Lone Star* were firing the field guns. The fire from the Gatling gun stopped. She could hear the boom of the field guns as one fired, then the other, and she could hear the irregular crackling of rifle fire. The schooner heeled over and broke away from the *Lone Star,* in retreat.

The Gatling gun opened fire again. Apparently Henri had paused to reload it. The schooner's stern was toward the *Lone Star* now, and it was helplessly taking the fire of the Gatling gun and the two field guns. Jessie could see eruptions of splintered wood as the cannonballs from the field guns tore through its superstructure. Suddenly a part of its forward mast came down, toppling into the sea, heeling the schooner over into a list. With its aft sails shredded by fire from the Gatling gun and its foresails collapsed, the schooner was an immobile hulk.

It was evening before ships' boats from both the schooner and the *Lone Star* made the beach. The boats from the schooner, carrying twenty men or so, the survivors, came as prisoners, under the guns of the boats from the *Lone Star*. One of the *Lone Star*'s boats had stopped at the drifting hulk of the schooner and scuttled it by detonating a small charge in its hold. It was gone now. A litter of debris floating in the swells, being washed ashore by the surf, was all that was left of it.

Henri was in the first boat—elated, excited, self-congratulatory. He ran to Jessie and kissed her, and to Ki and Ortiz and shook their hands. They had prisoners to interrogate, he said. They would learn much this night, he promised.

Ortiz and his *rurales* took charge of the prisoners. He ordered them stripped, to be sure they carried no hidden weapons, and only when their clothes had been searched thoroughly did he allow each man a shirt and no more. Except for those who were wounded, for whom he offered what care he could, he herded the prisoners into a circle on the sand and set guards over them.

The captain of the schooner had not survived. He had died on the deck, in the deadly stream of bullets from the Gatling gun. His first mate was among the prisoners. Ortiz gave him a pair of trousers and led him to Jessie and Ki and Henri, where they sat together on the beach, sharing a simple meal of beans and bread and coffee.

The first mate was Portuguese, but he spoke a sort of English. He was fifty years old, a swarthy man missing a part of one ear and two fingers from his right hand. "Manuel be sailor," he declared. "Since boy, Manuel be sailor. Come on land never. Never." He cast an appraising eye on Jessie. "Except for woman," he added.

"You're a pirate," said Jessie.

The man shrugged. "Manuel be sail ship where captain say, where owner say, be do what they say." He raised his dark, heavy brows. "You be hang Manuel, huh?"

"Probably," said Jessie dryly. "Unless you want to help us."

Manuel shrugged again. "Ship be gone," he said. "Captain be dead." He frowned at Henri. "Devil gun." He nodded. "Devil gun. *Dio,* He be no forgive you for that."

"Who owned your ship, Manuel?" Jessie asked.

"Fat man, be wear white, gold watch. See him once. Name? I forget. Big name. Much words."

"Baron Otto vom und zum Heligendorf?"

Manuel grinned, showing gold teeth. "Yes," he said. "All that name. One man."

"You used your ship to attack and take other ships, didn't you?"

Manuel sighed, nodded. "Pirate."

"How many ships?" Henri asked.

Manuel counted on his fingers. "One . . . two . . . three . . . four! Four ship."

Henri shook his head. "Five."

"No. Four."

"A big one, a packet, on its way from Veracruz to Havana," said Henri. "Named *Sarah*."

Manuel shook his head. "No. That one be take by big-name man and his friends. They be take. Go on ship . . . uh, *passejero*. Take."

"Where is the *Sarah* now?" Jessie asked. "Where are the other ships?"

"Isla de Lobos," said Manuel.

"Where is that?"

"You no be hang Manuel, Manuel take you Isla de Lobos."

"I think it's an island off Honduras," said Juan. "Your ship's charts will show it."

"Show where ships wait?" Manuel asked slyly.

"The ships are to sail to Cuba," said Jessie. "When, Manuel?"

Manuel shook his head. "No sail maybe, now."

"Why not?"

He pointed at the *Lone Star*, lying offshore. "This ship was be for guns. Like devil gun, maybe. Many."

"Where are these guns?" asked Juan.

"Ship," said Manuel. "Meet ship, be take guns from ship, be take on this ship to Isla de Lobos."

"What ship?"

"Warship," said Manuel.

"A navy ship?" Jessie asked skeptically.

Manuel nodded.

"What navy?"

Manuel shrugged.

* * *

98

Questioning of some of the other prisoners confirmed what Manuel had said. The *Lone Star* and the schooner were to have made a rendezvous with a warship bringing a cargo of guns to the tiny, swamp-bordered bay at the tip of Yucatan. There the crew of the *Lone Star* were to have been abandoned, and the crew of the schooner would have sailed the *Lone Star* to Isla de Lobos. The delivery of those guns would have completed the arming of the small force that the baron and his confederates had assembled on the island. Shortly the expedition would have sailed for an invasion of Cuba.

"They mean to make the *Sarah* the flagship of their invasion fleet, I suppose," said Jessie. "A ship my father named for my mother," she added, struck by the irony.

"Who is going to stop them?" Henri asked. "It seems likely that that naval vessel bringing them arms is a ship of the United States Navy. If the *Lone Star* doesn't keep its rendezvous, one of the other ships will meet the naval ship later—as soon as the word gets to the baron. By the time we can get word to anyone who could interfere effectively, it will be too late."

"Except," said Ki, "that when the *Lone Star* sails into whatever harbor there is at Isla de Lobos, the baron and his crews will think it has made the rendezvous and is bringing the arms."

"If you think we can attack their five ships and all their men with twenty-five *rurales* and one Gatling gun, you are being foolish, my friend," said Ortiz.

"I've been thinking," said Ki, "of their catapult, the way they expected to shoot dynamite bombs at us. We can do that. We have the Gatling gun and two field guns. We will have surprise on our side. We can do much."

"Against hundreds of men?"

"Do they have hundreds?" Jessie asked. "Much more likely, they expect to arm Cubans when they go ashore."

"Then why have they seized five ships? Two would have carried all their men, if they are so few."

Susan, who had been listening quietly, now spoke. "They plan several landings in Cuba," she said. "For each one, they will send a ship with arms and a few men to organize and lead. I heard my father and the baron talking about it. They will make their landings on the south coast, staying away from the Florida Strait."

"Well, how many men do they have, then?" Jessie asked.

"I don't know. They have Europeans, South Americans, North Americans—criminals, renegades, hired killers."

"What about sailors?" Ortiz asked.

"You've seen some of the baron's men," said Susan. "With a few of that kind on board—and in charge of all the guns—the sailors will do as they're told."

"And will jump to our side the first chance they get," said Jessie.

Ortiz shook his head. "You mean to do this thing?" he asked.

"If this gang of killers invades Cuba, overthrows the Spanish colonial government there, and sets up its own regime, who is safe?" Jessie asked. "Mexico? Imagine the baron and his confederates with an entire small nation in their hands."

"We must remember," Ki said, "that the baron represents an international business cartel, of which he is only one member. That cartel, in control of Cuba, would look around for other countries to seize. You have seen how they are willing to kill to gain their ends."

"But we are so few," Ortiz protested again. "In a week we can have a hundred men, two hundred."

"And by the time we reach Isla de Lobos," said Jessie, "my five ships may be gone, carrying the baron and his men to Cuba. We have enough resources to stop them. We may be hurt in the process, but I think we have no choice."

The next day Jessie, Henri, Ki, and Susan went out to the *Lone Star* and boarded to explain to Captain Putnam where he was to sail next. They took along Manuel and five of the sailors from the schooner, who begged to be allowed to join them. The remaining pirates were left on the beach, in the charge of Juan and his *rurales,* who set off for Coatzacoalcos, where they would jail the prisoners, stable their horses, and — as Ortiz hoped — requisition supplies from the local garrison. The ship would sail into the river mouth there and pick them up the next morning.

★

Chapter 10

Jessie had not intended to take the captain's cabin aboard the *Lone Star*, but Captain Putnam had made it ready for her and offered it with such innocent pride that Jessie feared she would offend him if she refused. The low-ceilinged cabin was tiny and crowded with the captain's serviceable furniture: his bunk, his table and chairs, his sea trunk. The walls were white. A single round porthole offered light and ventilation. It was primitive accommodation, but luxurious compared to the few other cabins aboard. Ki and Henri were given the tiny cabin ordinarily shared by the first and second mates. The captain was distressed to see Susan. He had no cabin for her and apologetically suggested she would have to share with Jessie. The captain was a good Methodist, and his face tightened and his voice stopped for a moment when Jessie told him Henri would share with her, Susan with Ki.

Offended though he might be, Captain Putnam arranged for water to be heated in the galley stove and hauled to a round zinc tub in his cabin, so his ship's owner could bathe. Jessie was grateful, and when the door was closed and the captain and his cook had returned to the deck, she opened the door a crack and called Henri. He came in and knelt by the tub to wash her back, to scrub her with a sponge soaked in hot water and fragrant soap.

"In France," he said, "you will bathe in a tub big enough for paddling around a small canoe."

"In France?"

"Yes. In France."

She would let that pass without inquiring as to what he assumed. There would be time later to find out and to resolve whatever question his assumption raised.

For now it was pleasant to lie with him in bed again, even if the captain's bunk was a narrow one and the room was spartan. With gentle fingers he tested the bruises she had received in the explosion. Only two or three were painful.

"You are beautiful beyond all other women, Jessie," he said. He nuzzled in her blond pubic hair, inhaling the perfume of her womanhood. "You are more than beautiful. You are a mystery."

"What mystery do you see in me, Henri?" she asked.

"That a woman like you can be all you are, so strong of will, so, as we French say, *formidable*. To find in one woman the qualities of Catherine the Great and Madame DuBarry—ah!"

She held his stiff organ in one hand, and with a finger wet from her mouth she stirred his pinched-up foreskin and felt the blood surging all along the length of the shaft.

"And in the art of love . . ." he went on. "Ah, what have I been able to teach you? You have taught me. I admit it."

She smiled. "I have held something in reserve," she said.

"What could it be?"

Smiling, Jessie arched her back and thrust up her hips. "Do you know what the Arabs mean when they call a woman *kabbazah?*" she asked.

"That she can perform what we in France call *pompoir?* But surely, Jessie, you . . ."

Jessica nodded, and grinned.

"I have never experienced it," he whispered, awed.

104

She had him turn on his back, and she sat astride his hips, lowering herself and receiving the full length of him into her. The position introduced him deep. She sat there for a moment, savoring the fullness inside her.

"Are you comfortable, Henri?" she asked.

He nodded.

She tightened her inner muscles on him until he was in a warm, wet grip. He gasped. She sat still, moving nothing outside herself, tipping her head, smiling down at him, while inside she massaged his throbbing shaft with a ferment of twisting, squeezing, pulling motions of her constrictor muscles. The old geisha had taught her this, telling her that only a few geishas exercised and developed the muscles and the control it required. Myobu had encouraged her to practice when she was alone, putting her inner muscles through the movements she taught her, until eventually she felt them strengthen and give her this very special ability. She sensed that Henri was about to climax, and she eased on him and let him slip back a little; then, when she felt his throbbing slow, she returned him to the peak. He lay speechless, breathing through his mouth, his face shining pink. She brought him to the edge again, and again let him slip back just a little. He closed his eyes and let her govern him absolutely.

She enjoyed this element of it—the power she felt she had over him. But, as Myobu had promised, her own sensations were exquisite. His manhood was swollen to as great a size as was possible for it, and it filled her tight. She experienced two climaxes of her own, each complete and satisfying, before she brought him to his. His was, as she had known it would be, the deepest, most sustained, most complete of his life.

When Ortiz rejoined them at Coatzacoalcos, he brought eleven more soldiers and the promised supplies of ammunition—including, fortunately, a case of ammunition for the Gatling gun—and, as Ki had requested, two cases of dynamite with caps and fuses.

The ship sailed, oddly it seemed, north, to make the turn

around the Peninsula of Yucatan. On deck, avoiding the stifling heat of the tiny cabins, Ki worked with the ship's carpenter to devise the method he would use to shoot dynamite-laden arrows. His task attracted the interest of Captain Putnam, who found some similarity between Ki's problem and his work of many years ago as a harpoonist on a Boston whaler. The three men worked together, trying one experiment and another.

Ki shortly gave up the idea of building a catapult like the one the Germans had meant to use to kill Jessica. It would be too bulky, he thought, and too slow—even if they could build such a machine with the limited resources aboard the ship. He concluded that his own strong Japanese bow was the best device for launching his arrows. It was shortly plain, though, that an arrow with two sticks bound to it was too ungainly to be shot any distance with any accuracy, while an arrow with one stick attached was so unbalanced that it wobbled in the air and veered off course. In the end he decided the only way to construct the arrows was to punch them through the sticks of dynamite, end to end. The captain and the carpenter could hardly believe what they saw, but Ki knew that a stick of dynamite was nothing but a stiff paper tube filled with soft, porous clay soaked with nitroglycerine. He knew he could shove an arrow through it without detonating it. He removed the steel head of the arrow and gently pushed it through a stick of dynamite, from one end to the other. Bound in place, it did not unbalance the arrow, and he would be able to shoot at least a hundred yards with all the accuracy he would require.

The ship's carpenter made him two dozen long arrows, each fitted with small lead bands at the head to overcome the imbalance caused by the stick of dynamite. Ki fixed fuses into blasting caps and carefully inserted one in a stick of dynamite pierced end to end with one of the new long arrows. Then he bound the fuse to the shaft of the arrow, and was ready for a test.

With almost everyone aboard the *Lone Star* watching, he carried his long, irregularly curved Japanese bow to the forecastle deck and prepared to fire an arrow to starboard.

He put a small kerosene torch down on the deck, since a match would not light a fuse in the wind. He strung his bow and tested it. It was a strong bow, and it required a strong arm to draw it. He tested the arrow on the bow, notching it, drawing the bow to be sure the stick of dynamite would not interfere with releasing the arrow. He was ready. He nodded to the ship's company, nervously watching.

When he lit the fuse, he must fire immediately. He touched the fuse to the flame on the kerosene torch. It fizzed angrily. He notched the arrow, drew the bow, raised it, and fired. The arrow rose in a long arc, trailing a wisp of white smoke from the fuse. The arrow began to fall toward the water. But short of the water the dynamite exploded in a flash and a puff of smoke, and the force of the blast blew back against the ship and through the rigging.

The test was a success. Ki had a new weapon.

Three days out of Coatzacoalcos they spotted a streamer of black smoke on the horizon. Both Jessie and Ki had been aboard steam-powered ships, but they were encountered on the ocean usually, not in the Gulf of Mexico. For most of a day they watched the plume of smoke grow as the ship, sailing east, followed a course toward the northern tip of the Peninsula of Yucatan—a course roughly converging with that of the *Lone Star*. Late in the day the ship drew ahead of them; shortly it would sail out of sight.

Jessie and Captain Putnam stood on the poop, studying the steamship through their telescopes. She was a full-rigged ship, with three masts and a full complement of sails that were now furled. The black coal smoke rose from a stubby, fat smokestack amidships. The smokestack, guyed with chains, was the only element of the ship that was not sleek. Her long, low black hull sliced through the water, throwing up a white bow wave. She flew the ensign of the United States.

"On her way to a rendezvous with the *Lone Star*," said Jessie. It's too bad we couldn't keep that rendezvous and let her have a taste of our weapons. With surprise..."

"I could not obey your order to attack her, Miss Starbuck," said Captain Putnam. "Look at the guns."

Jessie could see them through her telescope: two huge black guns, mounted on steel tracks on the deck, which enabled them to turn quickly to any point of the compass. Either one of them could fire a single shell that would destroy the *Lone Star*. Besides those, the ship was armed with stationary cannon that were visible through her gun ports.

"Even if she is being used for now for a criminal purpose, as ordered by criminal politicians," said Captain Putnam, "she is a ship of the United States Navy, and I could not attack her. I have no doubt her officers think they are carrying arms for a legitimate purpose, to be delivered to honest men. They would defend her with everything at their command and sink us easily. Anyway, I would not want to kill any of those officers and men. They are our countrymen, serving our country."

"You are right, Captain," said Jessie.

The warship passed beyond their view before sunset. Even the plume of black smoke disappeared over the horizon.

About noon the next day, the *Lone Star* passed by Cabo Catoche, the point of the Yucatan Peninsula. The warship was in the bay there, they had no doubt, but she was out of sight. The *Lone Star* held out to sea, outside the islands along the western coast of the peninsula, and bore southward toward the Gulf of Honduras.

It was too hot belowdecks to take their meals there, and they sat for their dinner around a table the captain had set up on the poopdeck. They invited Manuel to join them, and when they had cleared away their plates and cups they spread a large sheet of paper on the table and asked him to draw a map of Isla de Lobos.

"Be much sand," he said. "Be no water for drink. Must carry water for drink, on ships. Be no for eat. Must carry for eat, on ships. Be trees, here." He drew trees with hasty marks in the center of the irregular shape he had drawn for the island. "Be houses." He drew squares on what he had said was the eastern, leeward side of the island. "Man be make houses. Ships. Ships here." He pointed to an inlet he had drawn, again on the lee side of the island. "Ships be go, come. Bring water, food, also guns, more men. Bad place. Hot. Bad man. Much shoot. Much drink wine. I not like this place."

The ship's chart showed the island, south of the mouth of the River Belize and off the mountainous middle of the British colony. The chart showed it as the largest of a small group of uninhabited sand islands, protected on the north and east by a reef. The chart showed an inlet on the southeast coast, large enough for ocean-going ships to enter and perhaps shelter in a storm. The chart warned that there was no fresh water on the island, no source of food.

"There would be no reason to go there," said Captain Putnam. "You'd stay away from those reefs if you were smart. You couldn't go in for water. It looks like a perfect place to hide pirated ships for a short while, the perfect place to assemble a gang of hoodlums for the invasion of some small country."

"They'll be expecting the *Lone Star*," said Jessie. "We can sail right in and open fire. The trouble is, if we're hit by a few unlucky shots, we could be at a terrible disadvantage. Do you suppose, Captain, you could put some of us ashore on the western side of the island at night? We could attack from both sides then."

Captain Putnam looked at his chart. "Yes. We could launch the boats offshore and send some of you in for a land attack. You've got about four miles of island to cross, to make it to what Manuel calls 'houses.' I figure those are shacks and maybe some tents."

"If we surprise them," said Jessie, "we can win the fight for sure. If we don't surprise them, it will be tough."

"What if we must damage, even sink, some of the Star-buck ships?" the captain asked.

She merely shrugged.

All day the next day they sailed southward keeping an eye on an angry black storm that built up in the Caribbean, which sea they had now entered. Fortunately the storm passed to the northeast, toward the southern coast of Cuba, and all they felt of it was a cold wind, against which they had to tack most of the day. Toward the end of the day they began to see islands to their right, sandy cays protected by reefs, and they had a chance to study the kind of island where they must land. They were forbidding, flat, offering a home to nothing but a few birds. Such an island, Ki observed, would offer no concealment as they crossed its flat sand toward the enemy camp. They must, he suggested, land at night and make their way toward their attack under cover of darkness. It would be best if the *Lone Star* entered the inlet at dawn and opened fire as soon as possible. Then the land party would open fire. Everyone agreed to that plan.

Susan constantly invited him to lie with her in their tiny, stifling cabin. Even at night it was too hot there, and what sleep he got he got on deck, after he had left her. He wanted to be alone. He took out all his *shuriken* and rubbed them free of the slight spots of rust that had accumulated on this sea voyage. He tested his bow repeatedly. He unwrapped and rewrapped the bindings that held the dynamite and fuses tightly in place on his arrows. He watched Ortiz training his *rurales,* checking their weapons, choosing those who would go ashore and those who would fight from the ship. He wanted Susan to stay aboard, preferably in her cabin, during the fight, but she insisted she would go ashore.

"It is the baron who killed my father, really," she said. "He corrupted him and made our family hate each other. I will go ashore with you and do whatever I can."

He decided he would not oppose her. To do so would be to oppose a fate that awaited her, whatever that might be.

Captain Putnam was a skillful sailor, and he navigated and used the changing Caribbean winds so knowledgeably that the *Lone Star* came in sight of Isla de Lobos—the Island of Wolves—just before sunset. He brought the ship to the island from the north and west, on the side opposite the inlet and the camp. As he sailed down the western side of the island, they could study it with their glasses, and to anyone who saw them from the island they were an unidentified ship, hard to see against the setting sun.

The island was much as they had expected it—low, sandy, offering little concealment. From the west they could see nothing of the camp or even of the tall-masted ships that lay in the inlet. The land rose a bit in the middle of the island; otherwise it was flat. On that central rise grew a few palm trees, a little sparse vegetation.

The ship's crew began to prepare two boats to be lowered. They were lucky that the sea was not running high. He remembered the famous story told him when he was a boy of how the Mongols came to invade Japan and how, when they were offshore like this, making ready to land, the Divine Wind, the *kamikaze*, came to scatter the Mongol boats and drown the soldiers of the great Khan before they could storm ashore.

Ki would go ashore in the first boat, accompanied by Ortiz and Manuel and six *rurales*. The second boat would bring eight more soldiers. The first boat, returning to the ship, would bring Jessie and Susan and more soldiers. The boats would go back and forth until they had brought ashore a party of twenty-five. Then the ship would sail away to the north, leaving them on shore. If they were discovered in the night they would surely die, and nothing could be done from the sea to save them. He wondered if the baron required his men to guard all the shores of the island.

The last light of the sun faded. A thin moon stood above the sea to the east. The island all but disappeared, diminishing in their sight to nothing but a faintly darker shadow against the gray darkness of the water.

On the poopdeck, Henri Derval kissed Jessie fervently. Ki turned away and watched the first boat lowered to the water. Suddenly Jessie was at his side, seizing his hand.

"We'll do it," she said quietly. "There's not much you and I can't do together, Ki."

★

Chapter 11

Crouching in the front of the boat, which pitched and heaved even in this light sea, Ki peered ahead at the low shadow of the island. Juan was beside him. Behind, two of the soldiers had become seasick and were vomiting over the side. The sailors, rowing rhythmically, made scornful comments, but the soldiers understood only Spanish and would have been unable to object anyway.

"You have made it absolutely clear to them," Ki said quietly to Ortiz, "that they are not to fire a shot before the attack begins. Not a single shot. It would bring the whole gang across the island."

"I have told them," Ortiz replied placidly, "that I will personally slit the throat of any man who fires a shot before the order is given."

Manuel, crouched just behind Ki and Juan, touched up the edge of his knife with a small stone. "Be no lights," he said to Ki.

Ki nodded. They could be grateful they saw no lights on this side of the island.

At points the sea glowed faintly, alive with tiny phos-

113

phorescent creatures. They heard the splash of a fish. Ki wondered if these waters were not also alive with sharks. He looked back toward the ship. He could not see it, and he wondered how the sailors would row back and return with another boatload of the land party. He wondered, too, how they would find the same landing point on the beach and bring the rest of the soldiers and Jessie and Susan to the same place. Captain Putnam had assured him they could, without anyone showing lights to guide the steersmen.

The steersman of this boat spoke a command, and the sailors shipped their oars. This was according to plan, a pause just before they rowed into the surf, to listen for sounds from the beach. Ki strained, but heard nothing more than the waves crashing on the sand. It was strange how, even in the darkness, he could see the surf breaking. It broke less than fifty yards ahead. He could smell the beach, smell the thousands of creatures and plants that washed up and rotted.

The steerman spoke again, and again the sailors dipped and pulled on their oars. The boat began to rise now on waves that were dragging the bottom and beginning to turn over. It rose on one and rushed down its face, then was overtaken by another and lifted again. It lurched crazily forward, and in a moment a wave carried it onto the beach, and it crunched onto the sand and tipped.

The soldiers spilled out, most on their feet, some not, and scrambled out of the water. Juan rushed up the beach, beckoning them to follow him. Shortly they were established, ashore and crouching on the sand. Ki trotted ahead of them, up the slope and over a lip, onto the flat, dry land surface of the island. He dropped to his hands and knees and searched the darkness for sight or sound.

The night was dead still. The land where he crouched was sandy, but there was a thin covering of sere grass at this point. For an instant he was alarmed by the tiny, hurrying footsteps of some small creature scampering through the sand; but he heard nothing else, and he saw nothing. Apparently the first boat had come ashore undetected.

Ki slipped back over the lip and returned to Ortiz and the *rurales*.

"It is all right so far," he said quietly.

Ortiz pointed out to sea. "The second boat," he said.

For a moment Ki watched the second boat approaching, its oars slowly and rhythmically rising and falling.

"It is important," said Ki, "for us to know the land we have to cover. I will go across the island as far as I dare. I will return well before dawn."

"If you do not?" asked Juan.

"Then we will have lost the advantage of surprise. Fire the red rocket."

The red rocket was the signal to Captain Putnam and Henri Derval that they had been discovered, that surprise had been lost, and that the *Lone Star* should return to this beach and try to pick up the land party—or its survivors.

"Good luck, my friend," said Ortiz.

Ki shook Juan's hand. Then he trotted up the beach, heaved himself over the lip, and set out to the east, toward the inlet and the camp established by the baron and his gang.

The sliver of moon rose as he crossed the island. It provided a dim light over the bleak landscape, not enough to see guards from the camp—and not enough, probably, for them to see him—yet enough to afford him an outline of the land. The island was four miles wide. He had eight miles, then, to travel in the next few hours. Twelve, actually—because he had to return to the beach and guide the land party to within attacking distance of the camp, before dawn. He hurried. He wanted time to crawl around the perimeter of the camp, to learn as much as he could about how many men the baron had, and what weapons, before he had to start back.

In a short time he came in sight of the grove of trees that constituted the only relief to the island's bleak, flat sand. The grove was at the high point of the island, maybe as much as twenty feet above sea level, and in daytime it probably afforded a view of most of the island. If the baron was taking any precautions at all, he would have guards posted there. Ki slowed down and approached the little cluster of palm trees with great care.

His master, Sensei Hirata, had taught him years ago the art of approaching an enemy in silence and unobserved. He crossed the sandy ground toward the grove like a fluid shadow. If an eye spotted a movement in the shadowy moonlight, when it looked again to check, Ki would be gone, moved on. He was barefoot. He wore his leather vest and black pants. He traveled light.

The Baron Otto vom und zum Heligendorf was no fool. He had stationed guards in the little stand of trees on the island's high point. The guards themselves *were* fools. One of them struck a match to light a cigar and let a bright yellow flame glow on the night for a long moment. He could as well have beaten a drum to declare his presence. Ki slipped close enough to ascertain that there were two of them, two men wearing pistols on low-slung belts. He could have disposed of both of them easily, but he decided it would be a mistake. If others came to relieve them and found them dead or unconscious, it would be as much an alarm as if he had brought a rifle and shot them down from outside the grove. He decided to leave these sentries until he returned.

Moving on east, he began soon to hear the sounds of the force the baron had assembled. Like ruffians in a Texas cow town, they were drinking and gambling and fighting, and loudly laughing or cursing the fate that had brought them to Isla de Lobos. The camp was lighted. He could see the glow of lanterns.

Sound and light traveled far on this flat, bleak island, and it was still a quarter of an hour before he reached the perimeter of the camp. Lying on his stomach on the back side of a dune, in thin, tough grass that was sharp to the touch, Ki surveyed the scene spread out before him.

It was appalling. Of the five ships that lay at anchor in the narrow, shallow lagoon on the southeast corner of the island, only one was lighted—the *Sarah*. The others lay dark, abandoned. The reason was easy enough to see. On the far side of the inlet, the sailors from those four ships were imprisoned inside a rude stockade. The stockade was fenced on one side, and for the rest the sailors were imprisoned by the lagoon and the sea. Some could swim, undoubtedly, but swimming would have brought them only out of the stockade itself, still prisoners on the island, where there was no food or water except that provided by the baron's men. Some lean-tos in the stockade offered meager shelter for the sailors. Outside the stockade, half a dozen other lean-tos apparently sheltered the gang of misfits assembled for the baron's tiny army. Other buildings were more substantial—a crude cabin that probably housed the baron himself, a cookshack, latrines, and a series of solid, low sheds that Ki guessed were for the supplies of arms and ammunition the baron was accumulating. The assembled force was larger than Jessie had supposed. The baron had probably two hundred men here—his own men, plus the sailors who would be forced to work the ships for him.

It was obvious that discipline was imposed and enforced. On a gallowslike rack in the center of the camp, three naked men hung from ropes tied around their wrists. On the other hand, what had become of Henri Derval's wine and brandy was easy to see—it was keeping scores of bored, angry men drunk and tractable until the time came for them to board the ships and sail off for their invasion of Cuba.

Ki saw one advantage in the layout—the stockade that imprisoned the sailors was apart from the rest of the camp. Then he saw another—few of the men wandering around were carrying guns. Their sidearms and ammunition were kept, apparently, on one of the sheds, apart from them, to prevent mutiny and to keep them from killing one another in drunken brawls. A few men were armed, and grimly patrolled the camp. They, he supposed, were the men who controlled the place for the baron. If his group attacked now, they would have confronted no more than fifty armed men.

Ki crawled over the dune and down its face toward the rear of the line of sheds. In the morning it would be important to direct the attack at the sheds to which these men would run to get their pistols and rifles. If he knew which shed that was, he could try to prevent them.

He crawled to within twenty feet of the rear wall of one of the sheds. It was a primitive building, a sort of roofed-over frame with walls partly of canvas. As he stared, trying to decide if he could approach the shed and maybe even enter it, a pair of men came strolling along the rear of the line of sheds. They carried rifles and lanterns.

Ki could not slither back up the face of the dune. He flattened himself and subdued his breathing.

The two men walked past. They were speaking a language he did not understand, not Spanish, and it didn't sound like German. They were grim, alert men, and they glanced sharply around them as they passed him. They did not see him.

When they turned at the end of the line of sheds and passed out of sight beyond the last shed, Ki trotted in a crouch to the rear wall of the nearest shed and slipped between it and the next shed. In the shadow there, he was confident he could not be seen. He crouched for a moment, examining the solid wood-and-canvas walls. He considered cutting a slit in the canvas and so entering one of the sheds, but he could not be sure there weren't men just inside. He had little time to decide what to do next.

"It jollies me. It really does jolly me."

Ki started. The voice, speaking English, was so near it was difficult to believe the man was not speaking to him. The voice came, actually, from just around the corner of the shed. Whoever was speaking was standing just in front of the building, and his voice carried between the two parallel walls. It was a rough voice, Texas-accented, the kind of voice Ki had become accustomed to hearing among the wranglers they hired to work the ranch.

"Who'd'a believed it, after all these years, I'd git to go ta Cubey an' git rich on a ship stole from ol' man Starbuck's gal? Looka them ships, wouldja! He owned them, an' half a' Texas, and who knows what all, and he got excited when we stole nothin' more than half a dozen his cows."

"I felt better when they said that gal was hung. She's like her ol' man, you ain't never seen the last when you make a enemy of her," said another voice.

"I'd like to put a bullet in her."

"Ha ha! I got sumpin' better'n that I'd like to put in her."

Listening, Ki studied the roofs of the two sheds. One had a forge in it, apparently, since a heavy iron stovepipe came out through the roof near the front. He unwrapped the *surushin* from around his middle. Aiming carefully, he tossed the lead weight with a swing. It whipped around the pipe, winding the cord around the pipe two or three times. He pulled. It did not slip. In one quick motion he hauled himself to the roof.

The two Texans were just below him. He could have reached down and touched their hats. They wore pistols. They were apparently among the trusted guardians of the camp. They were in fact guarding this shed, and he wondered what was in it. He pressed his eye to the gap in the roof, where the stovepipe came out. He could see nothing. He put his fingers in the gap and pulled up. The board squeaked but yielded. Now he could see.

He counted four huge wheeled cannons in the shed. The forge was being used to bend the steel tires for their big wooden wheels.

He jumped across the narrow gap to the next roof. The shed was roofed with canvas stretched over boards. With his *tanto*, the slender, curved-bladed knife he was carrying, he cut a slit and tore the canvas away. He pried up a board and looked down. This shed was filled with rifles, hundreds of them, standing in racks.

Lying flat on the roof, he surveyed the camp from a new vantage point. He saw now that someone had excavated a dugout a little distance from the camp. That would be where they stored the immense quantity of gunpowder they would need to fire those big cannon.

He knew enough. He crawled the length of the roof and peered down at the ground behind the sheds, where he had seen the two guards walk by. They were not in sight. He dropped, but before he landed he knew he had made an error. He heard the metallic double click of a hammer being drawn back, and as he landed he felt the muzzle of a pistol touch his ear.

"Thunk I heard somethin' on the roof." It was one of the two Texans who had been talking at their guard station in front of the shed with the forge. "B'lieve I know you, ol' pup. Yeah. You're the Starbuck Jap. That means *she's* somewheres around too, don't it? And like as not the ghost of ol' Alex hisself. Well, there's them as is gonna be pleased to know it. Jus' walk careful-like, ol' pup. You an' me's goin' a-callin' on the baron."

The Texan held his pistol to the base of Ki's skull and marched him down the rear of the line of sheds. Ki knew he had but a moment to move, and he made his move quickly. He let his body fall forward as if he had tripped, but as soon as his hands touched the sand, he threw his feet backward in a kick to the Texan's crotch. The Texan had given all his concentration to his pistol, to bringing the barrel down and aiming it at Ki again, and he had left himself utterly vulnerable to Ki's powerful kick. The man bent over, dropping his pistol. Ki could not let him scream. He chopped him hard on the temple, knocking him instantly unconscious.

Ki looked around. No one had seen what happened, but he now had a difficult problem. Someone would be looking for the Texan soon. Ki could not leave him for anyone to find. He picked up the man's pistol, stuck it in the waistband of his own trousers, and then hefted the man on his back. Ki was strong, but the man was heavy. Ki staggered to the sand dune beyond the camp and up its face. At the top, he threw the man down in the soft sand.

The solution to the problem was quite simple; all he had to do was kill the Texan. The man lay unconscious, and a simple chop to his throat would rupture the larnyx, collapsing it, and the man would quietly strangle. It was no more than the Texan would do to him if he could. Still, the man was unconscious, defenseless. Ki's master, Hirata, had taught him the *kakuto bugei,* the way of the samurai. Without the way, that stern code of honor, he would be nothing but a supremely skilled killer. He knelt over the Texan, lifted him again, and set out to walk the four miles back to the beach where Jessie and Juan and the soldiers waited.

He had another problem on the way. In the little stand of palm trees at the center of the island, two guards waited.

His back aching from the weight of the Texan, Ki returned to the vicinity of the grove. He put the Texan down on the sand and began again the slow, painstaking approach up the slope, crawling sometimes, then rising to trot forward a few steps, merging himself into the shadows, using them as his cover, moving, always moving, so he would be gone from any spot where his motion of a moment before had drawn the eyes of a guard.

The guards had been changed. His judgment had been correct. If he had eliminated the two former guards, these new arrivals would have been alarmed. The two on duty now were Europeans, one wearing a derby hat, one wearing a soft, floppy straw, both in open-collared white shirts, both wearing pistols and carrying rifles. One stood with his back to a tree trunk; the other sat on the ground nearby, smoking a clay pipe. They spoke in quiet tones, in German.

Ki had already decided that a *nunchaku* would be best for eliminating these two guards. The weapon consisted of two wands of heavy, polished wood, joined through holes in their ends by a tough double strand of woven horsehair. In the hands of a skilled user, it was a formidable weapon. The velocity imparted to the swing of one wand, through the correct motion of the other, brought it against a foe's body with force enough to break any bone. It had often been used against unskilled swordsmen, breaking their sword arms—after which the next stroke smashed their skulls. It was silent. It was fast. It was simple. Often it left a wound that could not be distinguished from that left by an ordinary club. Best of all, it was easily concealed; Ki kept this one in a special long pocket sewn inside his jeans, along his right thigh.

He studied the two men. He judged they were brave.

They would come out to meet him; he would not have to rush in on them.

A few yards from the outermost palm tree he crouched in the shadow of the rise. He picked up a handful of sand and tossed it a few feet.

"Was war das?" asked the sitting German.

"Nichts," said the other.

Ki tossed another handful.

"Zum Teufel!" grunted the sitting German. He stood.

"Setzen Sie sich," grunted the standing man. He worked the bolt action of his rifle to chamber a shell, and stepped out of the grove in the direction of the sound.

Ki crouched low as the man came toward him, holding the rifle ahead of him. He came slowly, carefully, looking around. Ki poised with his *nunchaku* and waited. The man's senses were good, and his instincts were better. He approached the place where the handfuls of sand had landed, but he searched the darkness for some distance around. Ki could see his face. In the darkness it was hard to tell, but Ki guessed the man was one of the Germans who had accompanied the baron to La Paz de Cristo, who had sat to one side in the office of the *alcalde* and sneered as Ki and Jessie were led into the room in chains.

"Was ist los?" asked the man among the trees.

"Immer mit der Ruhe," grunted the man with the rifle.

He had spoken just as his eyes caught sight of Ki, crouching no more than a yard from him. He did not see the quick, whipping motion of the *nunchaku*. He never saw it. The wand struck his leg with tremendous force, halfway between knee and ankle, breaking the tibia, causing excruciating pain. He grunted, moaned, and toppled forward, dropping his rifle and falling on it.

The second German ran toward Ki, pulling his pistol from its holster—and he reached Ki just in time to catch the force of the *nunchaku* directly across the bridge of his nose. He dropped as if he had been hit by a bullet in the head.

The first German rolled over, grabbing for his pistol. Ki swung a third time, and the blow struck the man on the side of the head, above the ear. Both men lay still, probably dead but out of action in any case.

Ki found the Texan where he had left him, unconscious but still alive. Once more he lifted the man and plodded off to the west, his feet dragging in the resisting sand. He had almost two more miles to go before he reached the beach, where he hoped Jessie had stayed waiting and not set off looking for him. He glanced at the moon from time to time. He judged he had time for a brief rest before he set out to the east again, leading the land party for the attack on the baron's camp. He would need that rest.

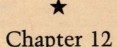

Chapter 12

An hour before dawn, when the moon had set and the night was black and starry, the land party left the beach and set out across Isla de Lobos toward the camp and the inlet and the five captive ships. Ortiz led twenty-seven *rurales,* a ragtag detail of white-clad Mexican soldiers. Jessie and Susan were beside Ortiz. Manuel, the Portuguese, followed a little behind, among the first soldiers. Again Ki trotted out a little ahead, to reconnoiter.

Ki had entrusted his long bow to Susan, and two of the soldiers carried his twenty dynamite arrows. He knew now where he would fire them. Jessie carried an extra Winchester for him. As long as the fighting remained long range, he might need it.

He hurried ahead. He wanted to be sure the two Germans still lay at the grove and had neither been discovered nor replaced. He wanted to assure himself, as much as he could, that no alarm had been given. Everything depended on surprise.

The two Germans lay where he had left them. The little stand of palms was deserted. Ki let the others catch up with him there, and they waited for the first signs of dawn.

As the first gray light showed on the eastern horizon, they could see the *Lone Star* off the island, slowly approaching the mouth of the lagoon where the other Starbuck ships lay. On shortened sail, the *Lone Star* tacked back and forth and made gradual progress past the tip of the reef and into the shallow water close in to Isla de Lobos.

The ship came on in silence. In three-quarters of an hour or so it would enter the inlet and proceed along the line of anchored ships toward the baron's camp. Jessie wondered if Captain Putnam and Henri Derval, studying the ships through their glasses, had come to the same conclusion Ki did that only the *Sarah* was manned. She wondered if they would see and understand the prison compound west of the inlet. It would be a tragedy if the ship fired on the captive sailors, failing to distinguish them from the baron's men.

As the ship glided smoothly into the inlet and entered the lagoon, the land party began a slow, cautious advance closer to the camp. As they came closer, they could see that dawn was the best time for their attack. The camp was quiet. Many men lay asleep on the ground. One poor devil hung naked by his wrists from a punishment rack, and through her glass she could see him restlessly tossing his head. She could also see that the camp was guarded. Armed men walked the perimeter. Others lounged about in the center. Two stood on a small pier built out into the lagoon and watched the *Lone Star* work its way in.

The ship was expertly worked. She watched the sailors in the rigging, shortening sail until none but two topsails remained to catch the wind and bring the ship slowly into position. It moved so slowly now that it hardly disturbed the placid inner waters of the lagoon. Though smaller than the *Sarah,* which it passed, the *Lone Star* was majestic in its entry.

"Jessie."

Ki was at her side. He touched her shoulder. She put down her glass and saw that he was pointing at two men walking out of the camp and coming toward them.

"Replacements for the two guards in the grove, I suppose," he said. "They'll see us."

She knew what that meant. He gestured to Ortiz and the soldiers to lie down, to conceal themselves as much as possible. He moved toward the two men, and she saw him dip into his vest pocket for a *shuriken*. He waited until one of the men stopped and pointed toward the little group of soldiers, obviously seeing them, and then he threw the star-shaped blade. She had seen him throw them hundreds of times, and he had even tried to teach her to do it. Still, the speed and deadly accuracy of the *shuriken* never ceased to amaze her. If the man saw it at all, he saw only a flash before it sliced through his throat. The second man had not even seen the soldiers. Ki's second *shuriken* buried itself in his throat, and he dropped silently to his knees, paused for a moment, and then fell across the inert body of his companion.

In the camp, a party of men had emerged from the one fairly solid hut and begun walking toward the little pier. She put up her telescope and looked at them. One was the baron, corpulent in white trousers, a white shirt, and a broad-brimmed white hat. He stood on the pier, waving a handkerchief.

The anchor splashed into the water from the bow of the *Lone Star*. The ship swung around. It would lie broadside to the camp, in the best position from which to fire the Gatling gun and the field guns, which still lay under the green tarpaulins.

Ki strung his bow, gathered some of his dynamite arrows, and hurried forward to within bowshot of the camp. Susan gathered the rest of his arrows and trotted after him. Jessie saw him tell her to go back, but she shook her head and stayed with him.

The men on the pier began now to lower themselves into a small rowboat tied to one of the pilings. They reached up and helped the baron into the boat. Obviously they meant to row out to the *Lone Star* and go aboard.

As the small boat approached the ship, a rocket whooshed up from the *Lone Star*'s foredeck. It was Henri's signal. The rocket climbed high above the lagoon and arced toward the camp, and suddenly, with a flash and a puff of smoke, it exploded. The report from the small dynamite bomb in the rocket reverberated across the lagoon and the camp.

Ki returned the signal. He fired the first of his arrows. It flew high, its fuse fizzing and trailing a thin line of white smoke in the still dawn air. It turned over at the height of its arc and plunged downward until it pierced the roof of one of the line of sheds that formed the back boundary of the camp. It disappeared into the shed, and for an instant Jessie wondered if the dynamite would explode. Then the flimsy wood and canvas shed erupted into the air, timber and shredded canvas flying in a fiery cloud. She could see why Ki had chosen to drop his first arrow into that shed. In the flying debris she could see rifles scattering as sticks across the ground or flying with the wood and canvas.

Ki had already loosed another arrow, and before the debris had settled from the first explosion, another shed exploded. Again, the flying debris included rifles.

Men poured out of other sheds in panic and confusion. All the men who had been asleep in the camp compound were on their feet, running and shouting. On the deck of the *Lone Star,* the Gatling gun opened fire. Men began to fall. Another of Ki's arrows exploded on the roof of a shed, making the shed collapse in ruin over whatever it had contained.

Many of the baron's men were plainly nothing but scum — petty criminals gathered from American towns and shipped to Isla de Lobos on a promise that they could fatten themselves on the spoils of a crime bigger than anything they could have imagined. Watching them run around, cursing in panic, Jessie could see that the baron had had little or no success in imposing any kind of discipline on them.

She watched other men with growing concern. Many others of the baron's gang were obviously trained soldiers who now, under fire, remained in command of themselves and were shouting orders to assemble a defense and counterattack. Many of the rifles scattered by the explosions were undamaged, just thrown out of the sheds; and some men were picking them up. In the wreckage of one of the sheds, a man was busy throwing out small boxes of ammunition.

One of Ki's arrows shattered against the wall of the solid little hut that was the baron's. The stick of dynamite fell to the ground and exploded, knocking in the rear wall of the hut and exposing the room inside. Jessie could see the baron's bed and his desk and table. Ki fired an arrow into the midst of a group of men. They scattered before the explosion, but three of them were knocked end over end on the ground.

Ortiz's *rurales* were firing now, sending a hail of rifle bullets into the camp. They were something the men in the camp knew how to deal with. They began to return fire, and bullets kicked up little spurts of sand along the long dune. Jessie sighted her Winchester on a man who knelt in the center of the camp, firing toward the deck of the *Lone Star*, and with her first shot she knocked him over.

The men who had been rowing the baron out to the ship had turned back. She saw the baron jump from the boat into the water near the dock, scramble ashore, and crawl toward the ruins of his hut. She fired at him, but he was sheltered by the walls, and she missed.

Under the command of a tall, shouting man in a derby hat, three men dragged an artillery piece out of one of the sheds and began turning it to fire on the *Lone Star*. A stream of bullets from the Gatling gun cut them down.

Others were running toward the dugout a little apart from the camp—their magazine, she supposed, the storehouse for ammunition and explosives. Ki saw them and fired an arrow toward the door of the magazine. It exploded outside the magazine, throwing up a cloud of sand but leaving the dugout undamaged. The men trying to go to the magazine fell back, though, retreating some distance.

Susan kept handing Ki arrows from where she knelt beside him on the ground. Between them, stuck into the sand, was the torch on which he lighted his fuses. The leaders in the camp compound had now determined where the explosive arrows were coming from, and one of them led a group of five men over the wreckage of one of the sheds and up the face of the dune toward Ki.

Ortiz saw the danger. He directed the fire from his soldiers at the group moving toward Ki. The five fell to their bellies, but they were not hit, and they aimed their pistols at Ki and Susan. Jessie stood and took aim with her Winchester. She hit one of the five. The others held. The bullets from the rifles of the *rurales* kicked up sand around them, but they held their places and tried to get off shots directly at Ki.

As Jessie watched, Ki lighted the fuse on one of his dynamite arrows. He had dropped his bow, and for a frighteningly long moment he held the arrow in his hand, calmly watching the sputtering fuse. As her fear rose to panic, he suddenly turned and tossed the arrow. The stick of dynamite had hardly landed before it exploded in the midst of the group of men. They disappeared in a geyser of smoke and flying sand. When, after a moment, the smoke cleared, Jessie could see them, all five, tossed across the face of the dune and lying twisted and broken.

Ki returned his attention to the magazine, which was being approached now by another party. He fired an arrow at the door. The door was surprisingly solid, and when the smoke and sand settled, it still stood. It hung loose on its hinges, though, and Ki fired another arrow immediately. The ensuing explosion knocked the door down.

The men approaching the magazine turned and ran. Ki's next arrow passed through the open door.

The very earth shuddered under the shock of the tremendous explosion in the magazine. Tons of sand, timbers, and other debris rose high in the air. The three sheds still standing, and the cookhouse and latrine, were swept aside by the shock wave that flashed across the camp, knocking men from their feet, knocking over the punishment rack and at last releasing the naked man, who staggered to his feet, shook off the ropes that had bound him, and ran away from the camp, out into the dunes beyond. The *Lone Star* shuddered and heeled. Bits of debris flew through its rigging, and some fell on the deck. The lagoon was dotted with small splashes of falling rubble.

The invasion of Cuba was defeated before it began. It was plain, less than fifteen minutes after the attack was launched, that the baron's purpose had been frustrated. His accumulated guns and ammunition were destroyed. The rendezvous with a naval vessel and the delivery of still more big guns had been prevented. The sailors who were to have sailed to Cuba now broke out of their compound and scattered along the beach. Many of the men were dead. Many were wounded.

Jessie trotted in a crouch to Ki's side. She knelt down beside him in the sand.

"Good work," she said.

Ki nodded, but he was solemn, thoughtful, absorbed.

She understood. They had defeated the baron's purpose, but they had not defeated the baron. He was still in command of a band of armed men, probably fifty, and they were slipping out of the besieged camp and northward along the shore of the inlet. Already most of them were out of the range of the Gatling gun, and Henri had ceased firing. They were out of the range of Ki's explosive arrows. They constituted now a force of disciplined armed men, probably stronger than Jessie's force, and the baron had several options as to what he would do.

Ortiz ordered the *rurales* forward. They had seen their enemy defeated, and with a shout they leaped to their feet and charged headlong down the face of the dune toward the wreckage of the camp. They had suffered no serious casualties—only three of them were wounded, and none of them had been killed—and now they rushed forward in the unnatural exultation of men with a sense of victory. In a moment they were out of control, and they charged over the wreckage of the baron's sheds, into the center of the camp, shooting down any man who raised a weapon against them.

Jessie would have preferred that they move on, pursuing the retreating baron and his gunmen, but the soldiers chose to pause in the camp, scattering through the wreckage, picking up guns better than their own, looting the corpses of money, watches, boots, and hats. They found the remnants of Henri Derval's stolen cargoes of wine and brandy, and soon they were dancing, lifting the bottles high and dashing the wine and brandy down their throats.

The baron and his survivors escaped. By the time Jessie and Ki entered the camp and walked to the crater where the magazine had been, the baron and his men had retreated out of sight, around the curve in the inlet. Probably they were hidden behind the hulls of the ships in the lagoon.

Henri came ashore with Captain Putnam. They too were exultant. Henri seized Jessie and kissed her fervently. No one had been wounded aboard the *Lone Star,* and Henri proclaimed that they had won a complete victory.

"Not complete," said Jessie. "The baron and as many as fifty of his men are loose on this island, well armed and ready to counterattack."

"If," said Ki solemnly, "we fail to reestablish order among our men very quickly, they may sweep down on us and impose on us a defeat worse than we did on them. A Gatling gun and dynamite arrows will have little value against an assault by fifty sharpshooters coming at us from the dunes all around."

"The answer," said Henri, "is simple. We gather the sailors who were held in that compound, board all the ships, and sail out of the inlet. We leave the baron and his hoodlums ashore on this island, with no food or water. They will surrender soon enough, to whoever comes for them."

Jessie nodded. "A good plan. But we must move fast."

Sailors from the *Lone Star* were sent along the eastern beach, shouting to the sailors freed from the compound to return to their ships. The *rurales,* whipped into order again by Ortiz, were set to work throwing all the rifles scattered in the camp onto a big wood fire, where they would be damaged beyond becoming again the arsenal for a cartel scheme. Parties of *rurales,* one under the command of the Portuguese, Manuel, ventured into the dunes outside the camp, to act as pickets, to warn the camp of the approach of any force the baron might put together.

"It is plain that their plan was more complex than simply the Cuban venture," said Henri to Jessie as the two of them

132

prowled through the wreckage of the baron's hut, examining his possessions and the few papers he had left behind.

"What do you have in mind?" she asked.

"They could have stolen anyone's ships for this expedition," said Henri. "They stole only Starbuck ships. They knew you would come looking for them, and they knew that would offer them more than one opportunity to kill you."

"I am afraid," said Jessie, "that is a major objective of the cartel. They killed my parents, and they want to kill me."

"The baron . . ."

"The baron is only one of them. His defeat has cost them dearly, and it will only make them more determined to kill Jessica Starbuck."

"I can shelter you from them—in France. I can place you beyond their reach."

"That's what my father thought. They killed my mother in Europe."

"They will not kill *you*, Jessie. This I promise."

Jessie did not respond. She understood what he had in mind, and it was deeply troubling to her.

Manuel ran into the camp. "Ship! Ship!" he yelled. He pointed at the row of ships in the inlet. "Ship! Ship!"

The third ship in the line was the *Sarah*. Sailors were in the rigging, hurriedly unfurling sails. Men on the windlass were raising the anchor.

"Man he be go behind ship," Manuel yelled. "Go aboard."

What was happening was suddenly obvious. The baron had led his remaining men around the north side of the lagoon, and somehow they had managed to board the *Sarah*. The sailors in the rigging were working with guns aimed at them from the decks. The *Sarah* was the biggest and fastest ship in the lagoon, and the only one manned, and the baron had seized it and was going to try to escape.

Jessie, Ki, Henri, and Susan ran to the small pier, from which they could see better. The great black anchor rose dripping from the water. The ship began very slowly to move forward, out of the line of ships and into the narrow open water of the inlet. As it moved into the open, they could see the baron's riflemen on the decks, threatening the crew, keeping the sailors at work. More sails dropped from the spars and filled with wind. The *Sarah* gained speed.

"To the *Lone Star!*" Henri shouted. He ran toward the little boat abandoned by the baron at the beginning of the attack. He reached the boat and turned and gestured wildly to the others to run after him and jump in the boat.

Jessie ran to him. "What are you going to do?" she demanded.

"The Gatling gun!" yelled Henri.

"No! You can't fire the Gatling gun at the *Sarah!* You'd kill the sailors."

"Maybe that is a risk we must take."

"No," she said with firm finality. "That is a risk we do not take, Henri."

"Then we must follow," he said. "We must not let that man escape."

They boarded the *Lone Star*, where Captain Putnam too had been watching in angry frustration as the *Sarah* turned its stern toward him and began to make headway down the channel toward the open sea.

"She's faster than the *Lone Star*," he said, pointing at the *Sarah*. "We don't dare fire on her, but we can't keep up with her either."

"Then they've escaped," said Jessie quietly.

"Maybe," said Captain Putnam.

"You think we have a chance?"

"Maybe," the captain said again. "Where do you think he'll go? Where would you be going if you were the baron?"

"Back to Europe," said Jessie.

"He won't go there in the *Sarah*," said Captain Putnam.

"Why not?" ,

"If you think he is," said the captain, "then I suggest I take you to Galveston. You can board a train there, and in a week you can be in New York. In New York you can board a steamship for Europe. You can be in any port you want in Europe weeks before the baron could sail there in the *Sarah*. She's a fine old ship, but she doesn't have the speed they have today, with steam to carry them against contrary winds when they face them. You can be in Europe weeks ahead of the baron—and have the authorities ready to take him when he lands."

Jessie nodded. "Then we can be sure the baron is not going to sail the *Sarah* all the way to Europe."

"That's what I was saying," said Captain Putnam.

"He'll go to Galveston, to the railhead, the same as we would do," she said.

"And since he sails in a faster ship," said Henri, "he arrives there before us and is gone before we can catch up."

"No," said Captain Putnam.

"No?"

"No. He has a problem. Unless my guess is dead wrong, the water tanks on the *Sarah* are empty. They have been hauling water here for all these men. My guess is that they used whatever fresh water was aboard the *Sarah*. The baron will have to put in somewhere and fill the tanks. But we have plenty of water on board for the voyage to Texas. That will just about cancel his advantage in speed."

"It is only a few miles to the mainland here," Henri objected. "How long could it take him to find his water and be on his way?"

Captain Putnam shook his head. "British Honduras is a Crown colony, well administered. If he puts in there, he will have to answer the questions the colonial officials put to him—whose ship is this, where are its papers, and all that. I don't think he'll risk it. I think he'll try to get his water in a Mexican town up the coast, and it may not be easy to take on enough water for fifty men and the ship's crew, for the month's voyage to Texas. Miss Starbuck, I think we have a good chance of reaching Galveston before the *Sarah*."

"Do *we* have enough water for the voyage?"

"We do if we don't bring all those Mexican soldiers with us."

They said goodbye to Captain Ortiz. He would remain on Isla de Lobos a few more hours, until he had finished rounding up all the sailors and a few of the baron's men who might have escaped during the battle. They would sail to the nearest port, in British Honduras, where the wounded would be put in hospitals and the ships would be provisioned and their water tanks filled. Then Ortiz would return to Veracruz in one Starbuck ship, while the others would sail for New Orleans.

"I wish you luck. You are brave people," said Ortiz solemnly. "I will never forget you, Jessie."

She smiled. "Particularly you won't forget the time you stripped me naked at La Paz de Cristo," she said.

Ortiz shook his head and grinned. "I will certainly not forget that," he said.

★

Chapter 13

It was all an immense risk. If their guess was wrong, their dismally uncomfortable voyage across the Gulf of Mexico to Galveston was time wasted. Through all that long voyage, Jessie worried about it. The Baron Otto vom und zum Heligendorf was guilty of many murders. He was a dangerous man. Worse, for Jessie, he had suffered a humiliating defeat at her hands, for which he would unquestionably be made to pay when he met with his confederates in the cartel. He might be fleeing now, returning to his estates in Bavaria to lick his wounds, but he would return someday soon— an embittered man under orders to destroy Jessica Starbuck at any cost. If their guess was wrong, he had escaped.

Their guess was not wrong. Standing on the deck of the *Lone Star*, anxiously studying Galveston Bay through Captain Putnam's long brass telescope, Jessie spied the *Sarah*. It was in port at Galveston, the only three-master there.

"We are too late, Captain," she said to Captain Putnam. "The *Sarah* is in port. They beat us here."

The captain nodded grimly. "So it seems," he said.

The *Lone Star* entered the bay and shortly dropped anchor. Jessie, Ki, Henri, and Susan hurried ashore.

None of them had ever been to Galveston before. It was as raw a town as any of them had ever seen—with the characteristics of a Texas frontier town combined with those of a small, poor seaport. The waterfront was lined with saloons and warehouses. Drunken sailors fought with drunken cowboys on the dusty streets. There was no hotel. Visitors could oust the whores from the rooms above the saloons and sleep in their beds—for the price of the best hotel in Dallas or Denver.

On the other hand, English—or a form of it—was the language spoken on the streets, and the rough, broken-nosed cowboys on the streets were Americans, and Jessie liked the look of them. It was an American town, a Texas town, and Jessie felt she knew it.

There was a telegraph office. She astounded the telegrapher by identifying herself as Jessica Starbuck and ordering wires sent to Starbuck offices all over the United States. She had been out of touch for entirely too long, and she knew her representatives would be relieved to hear from her. The single message she sent to all of the Starbuck offices was coded, and seemed only to be a report on the weather and accommodations in Galveston, followed by requests for information on various Starbuck operations; in fact it told them of the discovery of the missing ships and the identity of the man behind the piracy, and warned them to be on the lookout for the Baron Otto vom und zum Heligendorf, stressing the importance of intercepting him before he succeeded in escaping to Germany.

They took two rooms over the Gulf Star, the most respectable-looking of the saloons in town—rooms used ordinarily by the whores that worked the saloon. A twenty-dollar goldpiece moved the saloonkeeper to send cleaning women into the rooms, to tear off all the bedclothes, to wash other bedclothes in boiling water and lye soap and put them on the beds, and to scrub and air the rooms thoroughly.

The rooms adjoined. Jessie and Henri would take one, Ki and Susan the other.

They had voyaged all the way from Isla de Lobos on a ship where water was in short supply. They had had no baths. That was one thing the keeper of the Gulf Star could remedy. Not only was he able to offer hot baths in zinc tubs; he had long offered, as a specialty of the house, baths in which his house girls — for a price — joined dusty cowboys or salt-encrusted sailors in oversized tubs and scrubbed them until they were so distracted they forgot cleanliness in favor of things that interested them more. In these tubs, periodically replenished with buckets of hot water by teenaged bath girls, Jessie and Henri luxuriated for an hour in one tub and Ki and Susan frolicked in another. The little bath girls, naked but for simple skirts that ended at their knees, giggled as they poured water into the tubs; and while his special guests were still lying sleepily in the hot water, the saloonkeeper came in to ask if there was anything more he could do for their comfort.

When they returned to their room from the· tub, Jessie and Henri found a note, saying that Captain Cabell Baldwin, master of the *Sarah,* waited for Miss Starbuck in the bar. Jessie summoned a man from the saloon to tell Captain Baldwin to come up. She asked, too, for a bottle of the saloon's best whiskey.

Baldwin had been master of the *Sarah* on their voyage from New Orleans to Veracruz. He remained the bald, ruddy, severe man he had been — now a little haggard.

"Miss Starbuck," he said anxiously. "God be thanked, the ship is undamaged, and the crew is unharmed. God be thanked even more that you have come through all you have endured."

She let Henri and Captain Baldwin sit on the two chairs in the room, and she sat on the bed, wearing a full-length white robe she had carried in her trunk all the way from the ranch. The two men sipped sparingly at the harsh whiskey that was all the saloon offered.

"You are an excellent ship captain," said Jessie. "I value you, and you will retain your command and soon find promotion in our company. In this instance, though, I fear you have been *too* skilled."

"Indeed? How?"

Jessica sighed. "I had hoped to reach Galveston before you. I had hoped to be here waiting for the baron when you arrived. But you arrived here before we did. The baron has escaped us."

"Not so, necessarily," said Captain Baldwin.

"Not so?"

"The baron has had his problems," said Captain Baldwin. "In the first place, the men he brought aboard *Sarah* at Isla de Lobos were the scum of the earth, Miss Starbuck. Besides the baron himself, there were three other disciplined Germans—frightful men, capable almost of killing with a glance of their cold, cruel eyes. The rest had been scooped up from the gutter, Miss Starbuck. They were gunmen, killers, rustlers, gamblers, drunks—the absolute dregs of the West. Two of them were killed aboard ship—by their own kind, in gunfights over the smallest matters, a little money won or lost in gambling, an insulting word. When we put in at Campeche to take on water, almost half of them jumped ship and dispersed into the Yucatan. The Yucatan, Miss Starbuck! They thought their fortunes would be more favorable ashore in that forbidding jungle than in coming on to Texas with the ship. At that, their judgment may have been right. As soon as we dropped anchor here—which we did only late yesterday afternoon—the rest of them abandoned the baron. They robbed him first, took the money he was carrying. They were gone before the sun set, all of them. They left the baron and his three Germans on board. Just four of them. That's all that's left of the baron's army— just himself and three Germans."

"Nevertheless, they got away," said Jessie. "They caught a train . . ."

"No, Miss Starbuck," Captain Baldwin interrupted. "This is not Chicago. A train comes here only once every three days. The baron and his men did not take a train out of Galveston. When they saw the sails of the *Lone Star,* they left the ship in a hurry. But they took no train. The earliest train is tomorrow. Anyway, the train does not go from here, not from this island. You must cross to the north shore of Galveston Bay. The tracks go then to Beaumont and on to New Orleans."

The railroad had a ticket and freight agent in Galveston, nevertheless, and he was able to tell them no foreign gentlemen had bought tickets in the past week.

While Jessie and Henri were at the railroad office, Ki visited two livery stables. At the first he was told that no one had rented any horses or rigs this morning. At the second he encountered a man who did not want to talk.

"Git out o' here, Chinaman," the man said. He was a massive man, obviously his own blacksmith, with huge muscular shoulders and arms. He had no beard, but he was unshaven. He wore a leather apron over his trousers and held a hammer in his hand. He wore no shirt, and his glistening muscles rippled on his hairy chest.

Ki palmed a silver dollar and let the man see it. "I am prepared to pay for some information. After that, I might want to rent several horses."

"I rent to white men," the man growled.

"Cash in advance," said Ki.

The man prodded Ki's chest with his hammer. "I said git!"

"I am looking for four men," Ki went on, unperturbed. "They speak German ordinarily, so they speak English with an accent."

The blacksmith drew back his hammer, threatening. "You git outa here," he muttered. "Whilst you kin."

"Do you plan to hit me with the hammer?" Ki asked.

"Yeah, I plan to hit you with the hammer, if you ain't soon gone."

Ki sighed. "Try it. After you try, maybe then we can talk."

"Wha'd you say?"

"I said try it. Try to hit me with the hammer."

"Wull, shit! If that's the way you want it."

The blacksmith swung with his big hammer. Ki judged

the coming blow and could see the blacksmith had not swung for his head, not even very hard at his shoulder, where he meant the blow to strike. He was not a murderous man, just ill-tempered and accustomed to intimidating other men by his size and strength. Ki did not want to injure him. He ducked under the swinging hammer and came up when the man's arm was crossed over, pulled by the weight of the hammer, and chopped him across the nose.

The blacksmith rubbed his nose with the back of his hand and looked at the blood that came away.

"Wull, shit. You wanna rassle?"

Ki shook his head. "I only want to talk about horses."

The blacksmith grunted, spread his legs and arms, and came toward Ki. Ki threw himself under the man's outspread arms and dropped into a hard kick to the belly. The man took that blow and retreated a step.

"Wull, *shit!* You're a hell of a man for a little fella." The blacksmith rubbed his belly. "Okay, little fella. Yep, I did happen to rent some horses this morning, to three foreigners that talked funny. I took a big security deposit. I don't figure I'll ever see them horses agin."

"I'd like to *buy* four," said Ki. "First class. Good price."

"In gold," said the blacksmith.

"In gold," said Ki.

"We can deal, little fella. And later on I'd like to buy you a beer and rassle you a few falls. I still think I kin throw you. You got time?"

"Not today," said Ki, conceding the man a smile. "I would be honored after I have done my business and have the time."

The blacksmith laughed. "Show you what horses I got," he said. "You say you work for a woman? You need a rig for her?"

"Jessie will ride," said Ki.

"Sidesaddle? I got no sidesaddles."

"No," said Ki. Astride. Carrying a pistol in a holster and a Winchester in a scabbard. In fact, another of our party is a woman. She wears jeans, too, and will ride like a man."

"Them women I want to see," said the blacksmith.

142

"You will."

They walked through the man's stable, and Ki chose four horses and the necessary tack.

"I'll show you somethin', you bein' a cash customer and a tough little fighter," said the blacksmith. He reached into his pocket and brought out a red bandanna knotted tightly to form a little pouch. "Looka that. That's what them foreigners give me for the horses they took." He showed Ki a small diamond. "Them fellas didn't have no money, but that's what they did have. I took a chance. Reckon that little bitty thing is worth three horses?"

Ki squinted over the stone. "I would guess it's worth ten horses," he said.

"Hi-yee!" the blacksmith yelled, slapping his knee.

"But three, you say?" Ki asked. "We were informed there were four of these men."

The blacksmith shook his head emphatically. "Three, fer sure. A kind of fat one in fancy clothes. Two others. Mean-lookin' men, I do say. Dressed funny. I mean, dressed like dudes, only kinda ragged and dusty."

"How long ago did they leave here?"

"If you're after 'em, they got half a day's start on ya. More'n that. You got to git ferried off Galveston Island, and the last ferry has gone for today."

"If we pay enough, would the ferry make another trip?"

"Gladly. But he's on t'other side of the bay now, and won't be here till mornin'. Where you figger your three fellas wuz goin'?"

"To the railroad."

"No hurry, then. The train don't come in till noon tomorrow."

"They're impatient men," said Ki. "They might be riding on, instead of taking the train."

"To where? Beaumont? Not after nightfall they ain't. Them dudes ain't ridin' across this part of Texas in the night if they got a bit of sense. Even if you know this country, you don't do that. No, little fella. You ain't lost your dudes yet."

* * *

143

Ki reported his talk with the blacksmith to Jessie at the saloon. She, in the meantime, had inquired around town and had learned that the baron had sold one of his diamonds for cash to the keeper of another saloon. He had sold this one for one percent of its value. "Whut the hell good is it?" the saloonkeeper had asked, peering curiously at the gleaming stone. He had been happy to accept Jessica's offer of twice what he paid for it.

"We may as well get what sleep we can," Jessie said.

"I see no choice," said Henri.

"I see no reason for you and Susan to go with us," said Jessie. "It will be an exhausting, risky business. The baron is my enemy and Ki's, not yours, not Susan's."

"He's responsible for the death of my father," Susan protested.

"I will go," Henri said firmly.

"I am troubled by something," said Ki. "Why did one of the baron's men stay here? Where is he?"

"The baron's rear guard, you think?" asked Jessica.

Ki nodded. "I'm going to suggest we abandon these comfortable rooms we've rented at such cost."

After dark they slipped out of the saloon by a rear door and, keeping in the shadows, made their way to the livery stable, where, after a while, they were able to wake the big blacksmith. Jessie offered him twenty dollars for his room over the stable for the night—and for his silence—but he refused to take the money and offered her the room because, as he said, he had never seen so beautiful a lady. He would be happy, he said, to sleep in a stall in the stable.

Jessie and Henri took his room. The blacksmith pitched fresh straw into a box stall and spread blankets to make a bed for Ki and Susan. With a wink at Ki, he said he would sleep in the farthest stall down the line, so they wouldn't hear him snore.

They did hear him. They also heard the raucous night sounds of the town, even an occasional gunshot, and the constant shuffling and snorting of the horses in nearby stalls. Their stall was not dark. The moon shone through the high windows of the stable, and the reflection of yellow lights in nearby saloon windows added to the dim light that enabled Susan and Ki to see each other. She watched him soberly when he undressed—because he carefully laid out a selection of *shuriken* where they would be in instant reach. She pulled her .44 from its holster and laid it within reach on the edge of their blankets.

Susan's sexual appetite was almost insatiable. It was more of a surprise to her than it was to him. She said she guessed she was making up for lost time. She demanded that he plunge into her as soon as they were alone and naked, and she took him hungrily, rising to meet his thrusts with hers, urging him to go deeper, deeper, deeper. Afterward she scooted downward on the blankets, made herself comfortable with her head on his hips, and took his manhood into her mouth.

"I love to do this, Ki," she mumbled. "I love the way it feels in my mouth."

He bent his leg and slipped his big toe into her wet slit. He had discovered she loved that, too.

She moved her head up and down, sliding his shaft in and out of her mouth, between her cool lips. It was something she had learned to do almost entirely herself. She had an exquisite sense of what gave the male organ the most intense sensations. She had learned by experiment.

"Ki," she said, releasing him from her lips for a moment, "will Jessie marry Henri?"

"She has not mentioned any such idea to me. I would be surprised if she does."

"Why? He's handsome, rich..."

"I doubt, Susan, that he is as rich as she is. Jessie will never marry for money. She is not that kind of woman, and in any case she doesn't need it."

"But to live in a chateau in France! Ki, it would be heaven!"

"Jessie keeps firm personal control over all her business interests. She could not do that from a chateau in France, I am afraid. Anyway, she loves her ranch. It is her home."

"Maybe Henri would agree to live there part of the time.

If he were her husband, he could run her businesses for her."

"I don't think Jessie would ever give anyone control over her inheritance," said Ki. "The governor of Texas once suggested he would act as her trustee, run her businesses for her. She wouldn't hear of it."

Susan slipped her mouth down over him and took his shaft as deep into her throat as she could. She withdrew a little and for a minute massaged him all around with her tongue, then said, "And what of you, Ki? Would *you* like to live in France?"

"I will live where Jessie lives."

"That simple? Do you like Texas? It's so dull!"

"I have traveled much, Susan. I like living in Texas. I love the ranch. It has many pleasant memories for me."

"So that's it?" she asked. "That's the way your life is organized—permanently?"

"Yes."

Susan began to suck on him, tightening her lips over him, bringing him toward a climax. She worked on him with her tongue at the same time, and in a moment he came, filling her mouth.

After a moment she sat up. She sat looking down at his face, and she shook her head.

"Ki."

"Susan."

"I won't come to live on a ranch with you. I haven't seen enough of the world."

Ki nodded. "I know. I will miss you, but you are right."

They slept fitfully. The straw was comfortable enough, but the night was hot and filled with noises they did not know, which kept them alert for an intruder. It was difficult to keep any idea of what time it was when he was dozing and waking, dozing and waking again, so Ki had no idea what the hour was when the earth floor under them shuddered and the walls of the stable shook under the impact of a thunderous explosion. He jumped up, grabbing his pants,

146

and ran out to the street in front of the stable. The Gulf Star saloon had been blown away in a mighty blast. It was gone, and the wooden buildings to both sides of it had collapsed.

★

Chapter 14

"I see why y' wanted to sleep in my stable," said the big blacksmith ruefully. "Damn, I'm glad nobuddy knowed y' wuz here."

"You can see what kind of men we're dealing with," Jessie told him. "When the three of them rented horses from you and rode off, they left one man behind to kill us. Dynamite is one of their favorite weapons. This isn't the first time they've used it."

"He thinks you're dead, prob'ly."

"Let's hope so."

An hour remained before dawn, two hours before the ferry returned and they could cross with their horses to the mainland, so Jessie and Henri returned to the blacksmith's room over the stable, to sleep another hour. Susan lay down on the blankets and straw in the stall and went to sleep again. Ki sat half-awake and alert, with his back to one wall of the stall. He had an idea that the man who had blown up the saloon would come to this stable to rent a horse, to cross on the same ferry, and to catch up with the baron and the others somewhere near the railroad tracks. If he guessed right, and if he could capture the man, he could learn where the meeting was to take place.

The gray dawn light had begun to turn red when he heard the sound of booted feet walking into and through the stable. He watched through cracks in the wooden wall of the stall and saw the man walk past—a rather small but solidly built fellow, wearing a worn and dusty black suit and a short-billed cap. He wore a gunbelt outside his jacket.

The blacksmith had heard him too. "Who's there?" he asked from the stall where he had been sleeping.

"I vant a horse to rent."

Ki slipped out of the stall, jumped and caught hold of a beam, and quickly threw himself to the hayloft above the stable. He would jump down on the German, he thought. He would subdue him and then he could question him.

"I got no horses to rent," said the blacksmith.

"You have many."

"Those are taken. Already paid for."

"I pay you more."

"I don't want to do business with you, mister. You're the man that dynamited the Gulf Star saloon. You must have killed a lot of people."

"Dot is no concern of yours. I pay you vell for a horse. Get one out and saddle it."

"How do you pay me? With a diamond?"

"You know too much," said the German coldly.

In a sudden, fluid movement he drew his pistol and fired one shot. The blacksmith clutched his chest, grunted, and fell. Ki moved cautiously toward a spot above the German, making ready to leap down on him. The German turned. Maybe he had heard Ki, or maybe he hadn't, but he turned abruptly, alerted by something, glancing around with glittering cold eyes, holding his pistol ready. Suddenly his body jerked violently and the stable was filled with the sound of another shot. The German's mouth fell open, and he staggered. Then he was hit by another shot. He threw up his

150

arms, tossing his pistol in the air, and toppled backward and fell over the blacksmith.

Ki looked toward the box stall. Susan was standing in the door, still naked, holding the .44 they had given her in Mexico. She held the big revolver in both hands, pointing it down at the body of the German as if she were ready to fire again.

"No," said Ki. "He's dead."

"But I ain't, little fella," grunted the blacksmith. "Git a doc. Git Doc Crittenden, lives over the Gold Bull..."

The blacksmith would live. As the doctor worked over him, the big man told him and the town marshal what had happened.

"Anyways, you can't kill me with no little peashooter like this," he said, turning over in his hand the 7.65-millimeter Mauser the German had carried. "Souvenir," he said, stuffing it in his pocket.

Jessie, Ki, Henri, and Susan took the ferry across from Galveston to the Texas mainland. The railroad, they had been told, had been built only as far as the village of Houston, some twenty miles from the ferry landing. The train was due there at noon and would remain for an hour or two, depending on how long it took to unload and load the cars, and sometime in the afternoon it would leave for Beaumont, Lake Charles, Baton Rouge, and New Orleans.

There was a road between the landing and Houston, and they set off along that road, sharing the narrow, dusty track that wound among vast, deep mudholes with scores of wagons going in both directions, carrying commerce to and from the seaport. The wagons were loaded with hides and cotton going toward the port, and everything imaginable going the other way and destined for the ranchers of the hinterland. Herds of cattle were being driven toward the port too. They would be loaded aboard stinking ships and carried to slaughter to feed New Orleans. Farther than that, they could not be carried by sea.

Shortly, horses and riders were covered with dust. Jessie

slapped some of it off her with her hat, but it settled in a gritty layer, intruding even inside her clothes. She tied a bandanna tightly around her throat to keep it from going down inside her shirt. Susan tried to follow her example. Henri was probably the most uncomfortable. Still wearing a light suit—now stained and tattered—and a white shirt and cravat, he was hot. He had picked up a broad-brimmed hat in Galveston, so in that at least he was dressed for the country and even looked a little Texan. Jessie had bought rifles for him and Susan, which they carried in saddle scabbards. The blacksmith had equipped their horses well, with ropes hung on their saddles, though Jessie was the only one who knew how to use one.

"Is all of Texas like this?" Henri asked. "Something like this," said Jessie. "Wide-open country. It's a little more hilly near the Circle Star. It's indescribably beautiful."

Henri nodded, but it was plain he did not agree that Texas was beautiful.

They reached Houston late in the morning—a sun-baked, ramshackle village built around a little stockade that gave it its name. The few streets were like the road—both dusty and muddy. Recent rains, sweeping up from the Gulf, had flooded the town, and the dried mud soon churned up into choking dust. Some of the saloons and warehouses were separated from the street by small lakes of brown and green water, over which enterprising children had built plank bridges and were attempting to collect a penny toll from each crosser.

The local sign painter must have been a prosperous man. The fronts of wooden buildings were hung with a confusion of signs. It took some time to find the sign that advertised the ticket office for the railroad. Ki paid the children a nickel for passage for four across their plank bridge—and another nickel for holding their horses while they went inside.

The ticket agent was also the telegrapher. Jessie told him she would want to send several telegrams after they bought their tickets.

"I'm looking for three men," she said to the agent, an

152

old man with a tobacco-stained, gray-white beard. "Foreigners. One of them is heavyset and wearing a white suit."

"Yuh," said the agent. "Sold 'em tickets on this afternoon's train."

"To go how far?"

"N'Orleans," said the agent.

"Where would they be now?"

The old man shrugged. "Gotta be t' th' station 'fore long. That's out east of town, y' know. Build th' tracks on in, one of these days. But not yit."

They bought four tickets for New Orleans and arranged to have their horses carried in one of the cattle cars. Jessie telegraphed the Circle Star that she was boarding a train for Beaumont and points beyond and would wire information concerning her whereabouts when she could.

There was time to buy plates of beans and beef and cups of coffee before they rode out to the station. It was not far, only far enough to have saved the railroad the cost of building across the river valley. The station was not really a station. It was the railhead, with warehouses and cattle pens to either side of the tracks. It was noisy and dusty. They approached with caution, expecting to find the baron and his two German killers waiting for the train.

The baron was not there.

They searched the area. They inquired. No one had seen a man in a white suit.

"He's not staying in Houston, we can be sure," said Jessie.

"He is a wily man," said Henri, "and now he is on the run. Is it not possible that he rode on up the track, to board the train at the first or second stop?"

"To deceive us," she said. "To make us suppose he is not on the train."

"Maybe," said Ki, "he was watching for the man who tried to kill us last night—and instead he saw us ride in. Maybe he was watching in town, or maybe somewhere near here. He left the ship and hurried out of Galveston to avoid us. Maybe he has left Houston for the same reason."

"And maybe," said Susan, looking around nervously, "he left a man behind to kill us, the way he did in Galveston."

"That's always a possibility, Susan," Ki said to her.

"We have to check all possibilities," said Jessie.

"Meaning?" asked Susan.

"Meaning we must split up," said Jessie. "We must cover the train and the countryside along the tracks. Some of us must go on the train, and some of us must ride east."

"I will go on the train," said Ki. "Alone. The three of you should ride together."

"I don't like it," said Jessie, "but I don't see any choice. The baron is too clever. He may have found some way to hide on the train. He may have found some way to board between here and the first stop. The fact that we don't see him here doesn't really mean he can't be on the train."

"Once the train leaves here," said Ki, "it will travel faster than you can ride. You should leave now. I will stay and board the train. I will catch up with you soon enough."

"You are right," said Jessie. "I don't like it, but we'll take your suggestion. Be careful, Ki. Be very careful."

He told them to take his horse also. Then he stood in the dust, in the midst of a crowd of dusty Texas cowhands, and watched Jessie and Susan and Henri ride out.

He had put on his battered old Stetson, hoping that the shadow of its brim would help to disguise the unmistakably Oriental cast of his features. Instead of his favored footwear—a pair of rope-soled cotton slippers—he was wearing a scuffed, down-at-the-heels pair of low-topped Wellington boots. Under the circumstances, he did not wish to be recognized too readily, and it was his experience that this outfit, when he wore it in a crowd, tended to cause most people to mistake him for a Mexican or perhaps a half-breed Indian. Not that either of these racial types was universally welcomed in the West, but they were considered a part of the scenery and would not be likely to arouse the sort of undue curiosity that would attend a Japanese or Chinese. Ki allowed himself a slight smile at the notion held by so many white people that Orientals—or Indians or blacks or any other non-whites—"all look alike." He could remember the pictures of Caucasians that he had seen in Japanese books as a boy; all of them had had heavy beards, huge noses, and outrageously round, staring eyes. He supposed it was a universal trait of the ignorant to believe in such stereotypes, rather than to look at people as individuals.

Near the station was a saloon, and he walked inside to slake his thirst with a beer while he waited for the train.

They had looked into the saloon before. He knew the baron and his men were not in this crude place, an extended shack with a bar made of planks set up on barrels. There were no tables, no chairs. A poor-looking gambler tried to interest tired cowhands and wan ranchers in a game on the bar. One overaged and one underaged whore plied their trade. He heard the younger one explain to a youthful cowhand that she would service him out of doors behind the building, standing. If he wanted it fancy, she told him, he would have to go into town.

Ki ordered a beer and sipped it without enthusiasm. It was warm and flat. He knew better than to order whiskey in a place like this.

A tall, thin man stepped up to the bar beside Ki. "Hey, Cabe," he said to the bartender. "Looka this here. What you figger it is? What you figger it's worth?"

He rolled a diamond onto the plank bar.

The bald, sweaty bartender eyed the stone. He shrugged. "Piece a' busted glass," he said. "Ain't worth nothin'."

"No," said the tall man. "It's a dy-munt, worth mebbe ten dollars, mebbe more."

"Hell, Jake," sneered the bartender. "I won't give you a whiskey fer it, if that's what you had in mind."

Jake slapped a fifty-cent piece on the bar. "Gimme a bottle," he said.

"Excuse me," said Ki. "Do you want to sell that diamond?"

Jake looked at him skeptically. "Might be I do. Fer cash."

"For gold?" said Ki.

"You Mexican, ain't ye?" asked Jake. "You got gold?"

"A little," said Ki. "You say you think it's worth ten dollars?"

"Twenny," said Jake. "You got twenny?"

Ki nodded. "I might give you twenty. Maybe."

"Maybe?"

"Maybe," said Ki. "I have to know where you got it."

"Hain't stolen," said Jake roughly.

"I don't care if it is," said Ki calmly, shrugging. "Diamonds aren't usual in this country, though. Maybe it's like the bartender says. Maybe it's only a piece of glass. Depends on where you got it."

"Well, I got it from some foreign gent, if you must know," said Jake. "Said he was short of cash and had to sell his dymunt."

"How much did you give him for it?"

"Aw, I didn't give him no money for it. He wants me to do a little service for him, and he paid me."

"What service?"

Jake shook his head. "That's a secret."

"How can I guess what it's worth if you won't tell me what the gentleman bought with it?" Ki asked smoothly.

"Twenny dollars..." mused Jake.

"Maybe twenty-five."

"I never planned to do it, no matter," said Jake slyly. He grinned. "I cheated him."

"What did he want you to do?" Ki asked.

Jake glanced around. "Well... shoot somebuddy. Pot 'em with a rifle, from a ways off. Make no difference. The woman ain't here anyways."

"Woman?" Ki asked.

Jake nodded. "A woman. Yaller hair, good-lookin'. Wearin' pants like a man. Knock her off her horse, that's what the man wanted me to do. Shoot her. Hell, I wouldna done it. I took his dy-munt and *told* him I would, that's all. Twenny-five, y' say?"

Ki took coins from his pocket and handed them to the man. "Go back to town, Jake," he said. "What the man who gave you this stone didn't tell you was that if you had shot that woman, the people who work for her would have killed you within five minutes. Or they would have tracked you down if it took five years."

The train backed to the railhead. The old locomotive burned wood and chuffed dense white smoke and orange sparks. There were three passenger cars and five freight cars. As the cars moved slowly backward, impatient passengers jumped down and hurried off. A conductor at a window yelled and shook his fist, but still more passengers jumped off, some of them staggering drunk. Teamsters moved their wagons up to the freightcars, some of them so close they touched, the cars rubbing the wagons as they moved slowly backward.

Not sure that the baron and his men were not hidden somewhere in the area, awaiting their chance to board at the last moment unseen, Ki walked up and down the train on both sides, then through the passenger cars and back, three times. He checked the locomotive itself, climbing up for a moment to speak to the engineer and fireman. He warned them that dangerous killers were apt to board the train, either here or somewhere up the track. He could see they did not take him seriously.

Outbound passengers climbed aboard. Most of them were ranchers, lean and leathery and overworked and overworried. A few drummers sat together—salesmen of everything from boots to pianos. The gambler from the saloon sat down and stared moodily out the window, and Ki guessed he had made no money in Houston. Two women sat together in the first car. They were as lean and leathery as their men; they wore tall, broad-brimmed hats with their plain cotton dresses, and one of them wore a Colt .44 in a holster strapped around her middle. Two men in brushed black suits looked like undertakers but might have been cattle brokers or bankers. An elderly man with crutches propped up by his seat kept his face to the window and gasped asthmatically for fresh air. His son fussed over him like a wife.

"'Boo-ard! All a-boo-ard!"

Ki was satisfied that the baron had not boarded. If he was coming aboard this train, it would stop somewhere for him. As the train pulled out, he walked the length of each passenger car again. The baron definitely was not aboard.

The train was slower than he had expected. The land was flat, the locomotive had no grades to pull. Even so, it wheezed and strained, and only gradually did the train gather speed.

The countryside was piny and sandy. No road paralleled the tracks. Ki sat erect and alert, trying to keep an eye out on both sides. Most of the passengers soon dozed in the heat. He looked for Jessie and the others. He looked for the baron and his men. He didn't like the looks of the countryside. Too many pines. The baron could easily set up an ambush there. Jessie was careful and clever, but so was the baron.

The train stopped four times in the next two hours. At each stop, Ki watched the men who boarded. They were more of the leathery Texans, gaunt, stringy men with tired eyes. It was difficult, Ki knew, to wrest a living from this kind of country. Jessie owned the mortgages on a hundred ranches and let the ranchers have easy terms.

Two hours from the railhead he spotted Jessie and Susan and Henri, trotting along the track on the left. He moved across to a seat by the left window and leaned out. He waved at them as the train passed, and they waved back.

He was aware that someone had sat down beside him. He turned and found himself facing a pistol, held low and close to the man's body and so out of sight—and pointing up directly at his face.

"Be very quiet," the man said. "I know who you are, but I fear you do not know me. I am Reinhard von Driessel. Do not make the slightest move."

Ki glanced around. Reinhard von Driessel was the "son." The asthmatic "father" was erect now and no longer gasping. He smiled at Ki and raised a hand in salute.

"And the baron?" Ki asked.

Von Driessel smiled. "I fear, my Oriental friend, you will not have the pleasure of seeing him. That honor is reserved for the Starbuck whore."

Chapter 15

"In var," said von Driessel, "it gives many battles. It is bad to lose a battle, but vun battle lost does not a var lose. I could vish, Jappanner, dot you vere our side on. Ve have learned to respect you."

Von Driessel held his pistol close to his own vest, yet close to Ki's ribs—out of sight of the other passengers in the car. Ki could knock a pistol aside almost anytime one was pointed at him. Since he came to the United States and discovered that the pistol was every man's weapon, he had practiced for many hours on a sudden move that sprained a gunman's wrist and wrenched the pistol aside. It required, though, a moment's inattention by the gunman, and this professional killer was not going to be inattentive, even for an instant. Anway, the "father" had moved to a seat behind Ki, and Ki understood that another pistol was pointed at his back and could be fired through the seat.

"I know now how you got on the train without my seeing you," said Ki. "You rode out the track to the first stop, boarded there, and were already on the train when it backed into Houston."

161

Von Driessel smiled and nodded. "You are not the only smart vun, Japanner."

"I wonder how smart you are," said Ki. "Two of you are here. That means the baron is somewhere alone. Three of my people are watching for him. Likely he is at a stop up the line, and he will be alone when they find him."

The German's face darkened. "Two of dem are vomen," he said scornfully.

"Jessica Starbuck can ride and shoot as well as any man," said Ki. "And the girl with her is the one who shot your friend who stayed behind in Galveston to dynamite the saloon."

Von Driessel's smile returned. "It vill be three against three, actually, " he said. "Fritz and I vill be vith the baron. You will be dead, of course."

"Where?" Ki asked.

"At a town called Alexandra. About half an hour from here."

Ki glanced over his shoulder into the face of the other German, the one that von Driessel called Fritz. Having seen the faces of the two of them, he remembered what Captain Baldwin had said of them—that they might be able to kill with a glance of their cold, cruel eyes.

"So ve must do it, Japanner," said von Driessel with a sigh. "Not in ziss car. Dere are too many Texans vith guns here. In ze rear car. You walk ahead. Ve vill be behind."

Ki slid out of his seat and walked slowly through the aisle of the passenger car. Even if he saw a chance to attack, it would be too dangerous to do it here, where the bullets would fly among all these people. He turned the handle on the door and made the crossing into the next car, the last car on the train. There were not so many people there.

He had guessed what the two Germans meant to do. They were going to march him to the rear door of this last car, open it, and shoot him in the back. His body would fall to the tracks, and the people in the car might not even realize what had happened.

"Gents, do I have yer tickets?" called the old conductor from behind them. He had followed from the other car.

"Giff him your ticket," muttered von Driessel.

Ki reached into the pocket of his vest for his ticket. His hand there touched the steel of a *shuriken,* but there was no way to swing around and use it.

"You haff our tickets," said the German to the conductor.

The conductor nodded. He looked skeptically at Fritz. "Got yer health back quick, didn't ya?"

Prodded from behind, Ki walked the rest of the way to the end of the car. He turned the handle on the door and pretended to push.

"Locked," he said.

"Not locked," said von Driessel grimly. "Push!"

Ki gave the door a firm push and it swung open. He looked down at the tracks rushing away behind the train. The door swung out, then back, in the rushing air.

"Hey! You can't open that there door! They ain't—"

The two Germans glanced back in annoyance. It was the instant of distraction that Ki needed. He leaped for the door that swung out over the tracks, seized the top of it, and swung his legs up. With his knees over the top of the door, giving him a purchase, he threw his body into an upward lurch toward the roof of the car. His hands grabbed for the edge of the roof and caught hold, and he pulled himself quickly up, dealing von Driessel a kick in the face. Bullets shattered the wood and glass of the door, but Ki was already on top of the car.

He trotted forward, kicking off his Wellingtons for better traction and a more secure feel for the swaying motion of the car. Reaching the forward end of the car, he jumped easily across the gap to the roof of the next car and trotted forward across it.

He knew the two Germans could and would come up. They could come up anywhere, between any two cars, and if they were smart, one would try to come up ahead of him and one behind, to trap him between them. They *were* smart. That was what they would do. His defense was to work his way across all three passenger cars and onto the roof of the last freight car. They could not pass through the freight cars, so they could only come up behind him.

Obviously they had thought the same way, because before he could make his way all the distance forward to the front end of the front passenger car, a face appeared over the edge of the roof for an instant, followed by a pistol and a shot. The bullet whizzed by him. It was Fritz, and he had seen him and taken a chance on one quick, unaimed shot that might at least drive him back and keep him on this one car.

Fritz made an error. He poked his head up to have a look. Ki launched a *shuriken* in one lightning-fast flip, and the little blade sank itself in the German's forehead, just above an eyebrow. Fritz howled and slipped back, but Ki knew he was not taken out of the fight, only bloodied and angered and momentarily stunned. In that moment when the German was stunned, Ki jumped over his head, from the roof of the passenger car to the roof of the last freightcar, a yellow boxcar.

Ki ran forward on the roof of the swaying boxcar. At the forward end of the car he dropped from the roof, down between that car and the next, hanging on the ladder and brake wheel. A bullet chipped the edge of the roof. He risked a look over just the same and saw the two Germans coming, the one with blood running down his face and onto his clothes. Ki flipped a *shuriken*. In the whirling currents of air atop the moving cars, the little blade missed both men and sailed away into the air. Another bullet sang off the edge of the roof.

The two Germans were now on the forward edge of the first passenger car, Ki down between the last two freight cars. The train rolled northward, moving at maybe forty miles an hour, the cars rolling and swaying. Ki swung out to the side to see if he could move along the side of a boxcar. He saw he couldn't. There were grab-irons on the cars at the ends and in the center where the doors opened, but none between, and the jump would be too long. He looked underneath. On the undersides the cars were braced with long tie rods that ran from one end to the other. He had heard that men sometimes lay on those rods and rode the train that way, but from above, on a moving train, there was no way to get beneath a car. Again he risked a look above. Von Driessel and Fritz were crouched on the roof of the passenger car. For the moment the situation was stalemated.

He knew they would not leave it that way. He felt the shock of a small explosion atop the boxcar, and the debris whipped by. He looked over the top again. Dynamite again, though only part of a stick this time, in a small bomb. It had blown a hole in the roof of the car.

They would slide another one along the roof, he guessed. It would fall between the cars and explode in his face.

Ki lunged around the end of the boxcar and hung from the side, by the grab-irons. As he had expected, a bomb fell between the cars and exploded, blowing the flimsy wooden walls out of the front of one car, the rear of the other. One end of his grab-iron was anchored in a plank that was broken, and for a moment the grab-iron turned, and he thought he might fall. But it held. He swung back between the cars, pushed himself through the hole blown in the end, and dropped inside the boxcar.

The car was empty except for a few bales of smelly cowhides. He moved along the wall to the sliding doors, threw the lever that unlatched the doors, and pulled one of them open about two feet. Grabbing the track in which the doors hung, he lifted himself for a cautious look at the roof.

The Germans had rushed across the roof, to shoot down on him while he was stunned—if in fact the explosion had not knocked him off the car entirely. Von Driessel was on his knees, peering over the end of the car. Fritz was staring down through the hole in the roof and would have seen him inside the boxcar if he had not swung outside the doors.

Ki hung by one arm, fishing in his pocket for a blade to launch at Fritz, but the bloodied German turned away from the hole and walked directly toward him, as if he had seen him. Yet he had not seen him. He came within reach, and Ki lunged up and struck him with a sidehand chop to the knee. Fritz staggered, knocked off his balance, and Ki grabbed him by the pants leg and pulled hard. The German's eyes bulged in terror as he fell forward, flailing his arms in the air in a vain attempt to recover his balance. He fell silently. He fell past Ki and landed headfirst on the ties at the edge of the track. He bounced and cartwheeled along the roadbed, his blood flying.

"Fritz? Fritz? *Fritz!*"

Von Driessel looked over the side of the car just as Ki swung back inside.

"All right, Japanner. You're inside, are you? All right."

Through the hole in the roof the boxcar, Ki saw von Driessel jump to the roof of the car ahead. He anticipated what was coming. A moment after von Driessel jumped, a bomb with a sputtering fuse dropped through the hole in the roof and fell into the car. Even if Ki had meant to grab it and throw it out, he did not have that choice, because another bomb fell immediately after it.

He threw himself out the door, grabbing the lower door track to hang on to. He swung his body outward, his feet missing the rough, speeding ties underneath by inches, and swung back in, reaching with his toes for the tie rod. He caught it with one foot, and got enough purchase to let him catch it with the other foot. And there he hung under the floor of the car, his hands gripping the door track, his feet wedged in the nearer tie rod, when the two bombs went off in quick succession.

The floor was solid, but the walls and roof were flimsy. The force of the explosions blew out the side walls and part of the roof of the car, but the floor remained intact, with Ki hanging there, weakening, struggling somehow to improve his hold, the roadbed rushing under him.

Then he felt the brakes take hold, and the train slowed, and in a few hundred yards it lurched to a stop.

"Git back, folks! Git back in yer cars, please!"

The fireman from the locomotive trotted back along the cars, yelling at the passengers who had begun to jump down from their cars.

"What's goin' on?" demanded a big Texan.

"There's a crazy man up front in the locomotive," said the engineer. "He come across the top of the cars with a gun in his hand and dropped down on us, and he says he'll shoot Ed if we don't all do what he says. We stopped when he heard the explosions back here, but he wants to go on."

"What else he want you to do?" the Texan asked.

"Uncouple right here," said the fireman. He began to work on the coupling between the forward cars and the shattered boxcar. "This here car's so busted up, she'll be a drag on us. He wants her uncoupled. He says he'll shoot Ed if anybody tries to come on the train with us. Please, folks. Please go back to your cars!"

Ki waited until the fireman had returned to the locomotive, which began to huff and move the cars again, and then he seized the grab-irons on the rear of what was now the last freightcar and hauled himself aboard.

At the last moment the big Texan followed, grabbing the irons and lifting himself on the car. He was a man in his fifties, Ki judged—rawboned, sunburned, grim.

"You ain't got no gun, little fella," the Texan said to Ki. "Reckon you could use help. Anyways, I don't cotton to no crazy man stealin' the train I'm tryin' to get to Beaumont on."

"How far is it to Alexandra?" Ki asked.

The Texan glanced around. "Reckon not more'n a mile or two. Say, what's that crazy man doin'?"

He referred to the way the train was accelerating. The locomotive's drive wheels were screeching on the track, and the train gathered speed in a series of lurches. Ki climbed atop the boxcar and ran forward, leaping to the next car. The Texan followed, running slowly and awkwardly in his boots. By the time Ki reached the front of the first boxcar behind the tender, the Texan was still crossing the third car.

Ki dropped lightly onto the load of firewood in the tender. Carefully he climbed over the wood, peering over for a look at what was happening in the cab of the locomotive. He saw von Driessel at last, standing beside the engineer, holding a pistol directly to his head, glancing back and forth between him and the track ahead. He reached up and pulled the whistle cord. The whistle shrieked once and then again.

167

The German nudged the engineer, and the engineer eased back on the throttle. The village of Alexandra was ahead, less than a mile away.

Ki slipped a *shuriken* into the palm of his hand. If the baron was standing by the platform in Alexandra, Ki meant to kill him. If that opportunity was not there, then he would launch the blade at von Driessel, and this time he would not miss. He climbed a little higher on the load of wood.

"Hey! Hey, you crazy son of a bitch!"

The big Texan stood atop the first boxcar, at the edge of the roof. Von Driessel jerked around to fire a shot at him, and the Texan fired one first. The bullet hit one of the gauges on the rear of the locomotive's boiler, and a screech of steam burst out and scalded the back of the German's neck. Even so, von Driessel fired a shot at the Texan, and the Texan dropped to the roof of the boxcar to afford himself a little shelter and fired again.

The engineer, in a panic, staggered against the throttle. The locomotive whooshed wildly and lurched forward, again gaining speed with screeching wheels.

Ki jumped up to launch his *shuriken*, but the Texan's next shot whizzed by his ear, and he was forced to throw himself facedown in the firewood. He felt the train continuing to gain speed, and when he raised himself again he saw the tiny village of Alexandra. In fact, he saw the baron standing on the platform, ruddy, white-suited, stamping his foot in anger and frustration as the train sped past. The train had attained a tremendous speed now, maybe as much as sixty miles an hour—a crazy speed that was sure to make it fly from the tracks at the first curve. Von Driessel fired twice more at the Texan on the roof of the boxcar, and the Texan fired back. The engineer and fireman cowered on the floor, trying to shield themselves from the ricocheting bullets, and nobody was driving the train.

Ki hardly dared raise his head. Von Driessel must have reloaded, and the Texan must have also, because they fired more than six shots apiece. The Texan's bullets, striking the steel and cast iron of the locomotive cab, bounced wildly around, nicking von Driessel without really wounding him.

He was a wild man now. He had been cautious before, but now he stood and traded shots with the Texan, one after another, and it seemed to Ki that one of them must die shortly.

It would be better for him if it was von Driessel. He picked up a heavy piece of firewood. He saw his chance and heaved the quarter of a log at the German's face. Von Driessel was entirely unprepared for that, and the wood hit him full on the nose and staggered him backward.

"Ha!" yelled the Texan, and he stood, took aim, and shot von Driessel through the chest.

Ki scrambled off the woodpile and jumped into the cab. He pulled back on the throttle. The locomotive began to slow, and the engineer stood up and applied the brakes.

The Texan jumped down. "Wondered where *you* was," he said to Ki. "I was feared he'd got ya. Crazy man, warn't he? What the hell did he have in his head?"

"That's a long story," said Ki. He turned to the engineer. "We must go back to Alexandra as quickly as possible."

"Not so quick," the engineer said glumly.

"What do you mean?"

"Look at 'er," said the engineer. "She's leakin' steam from six or seven bullet holes."

He was right. Steam whistled through holes in pipes struck by bullets. The pressure gauge was going down.

"No, sir," said the engineer. "Can't go nowheres till she's patched up."

Ki leaned out of the cab as the locomotive came to a stop. He looked back.

"How far is it back to Alexandra?" he asked.

"Speed we wuz goin', got to figger three mile, four. Mebbe five even. How come yer in a big hurry to git there? Never knowed nobody wuz in no hurry to git to Alexandra."

Ki slumped in discouragement. "People I care for," he sighed, "are going to face another crazy man there."

"Got no horses in the cars?" asked the Texan.

The engineer shook his head.

Ki jumped down from the cab and set off running back along the track toward Alexandra.

Chapter 16

Jessie, Henri, and Susan galloped up to the stranded passenger cars and the blown-apart boxcar. Angry passengers stood around, still gesticulating and cursing.

"They was three crazy men on the train," said the old conductor. "Two blond ones with hard eyes and some kind of funny accents, and one Mex, I guess he was. Fer some reason the two blond ones wanted to kill the Mex, and they did about all they could for the purpose. Shot at 'im. Blowed up the boxcar. He got one of 'em, or one of 'em fell off; anyways, one of 'em must be dead, fallin' on the track the way he did. He—"

"He's dead," said Jessie. "We saw him back there. But what happened to the one you're calling a Mexican?"

"T'other blond one put a gun to the head of the engineer and tol' the fireman to come back and uncouple. Last I seed of the Mex, he jumped on the back of what was left of the train and rode off with it."

"George Simpson clumb on, too," said a Texan.

"The two blond men were Germans," said Jessie. "Are you sure there's not another one on the train—a heavyset

171

one, probably wearing a white suit?"

The conductor shook his head. "No. Say, who are you, anyways?" He eyed the two women clad in jeans with a skeptical eye, then looked over Henri. "Somebody's in big trouble for stealin' a train."

"I'm Jessica Starbuck."

"Starbuck? *The* Starbuck family?"

"Yes. Are you sure there's no other German aboard?"

"Look through the cars yerself, Miss Starbuck."

They did, but it was plain the baron had not been aboard the train. They rode on, following the tracks. The train was nowhere in sight.

"He's got to stop somewhere and pick up the baron," said Jessie.

"Ki has killed one of them. He'll kill the other," said Susan.

"Probably," said Jessie.

"But how far from Houston could the baron have ridden?" Henri asked. "We have ridden almost three hours..."

"He's had many more hours to ride," said Jessie. "His plan was to let his killers on the train have enough time to finish their work before he came aboard."

"And if they failed, not to come aboard at all," Henri suggested.

"Exactly. Which means he probably intends to board the train at a stop."

"Let us hope there is one soon," said Henri. "Our horses are tired if we are not, and very soon we must stop for rest and water."

A squat water tank beside the track was the first thing anyone saw of the town of Alexandra, coming from either direction. It was the tallest structure in town, made of wood staves and hooped like a vastly oversized wooden barrel, built high enough to pour water through a spout into the tank of a locomotive tender. The name of the town had once been painted on the tank, but the letters were now so faded as to be almost illegible. The tiny station was no more than a shack. A single street running perpendicular to the tracks

172

and stopping at the station was lined with two saloons, a general store, two weatherbeaten houses, and a small church.

A small cluster of men stood on the station platform, staring north. The train was not in sight.

Jessie urged her horse forward and galloped toward the rickety station platform. The men on the platform heard the hoofbeats of her horse, and in unison they turned, pulled pistols from their holsters and pockets, and opened fire on her.

Jessie reined in. Bullets were flying all around her. She leaped from her horse and threw herself prone on the sandy ground. She looked back. Henri and Susan had thrown themselves down. Their horses were running off in panic.

The gunfire was ragged and ill-aimed. Bullets whizzed overhead. Others kicked up sand. Still others struck rocks and ricocheted with a whine.

"Hey!" Jessie yelled. "What's the matter with you people? Stop shooting! Are you all crazy?"

The shooting petered out and raggedly stopped. The men stood on the platform, looking at her intently.

"You a woman, f' gosh sake?"

"Yes, I'm a woman," she yelled. "I'm Jessica Starbuck."

One of the men stepped off the edge of the platform and walked toward her. Shaggy, tattered, openmouthed, he stared at her and came closer.

"Starbuck?" he asked.

She stood, tossed her head to toss off her Stetson and let her blond hair fly, and nodded.

"Goddamn," the man said. He jerked around and stared at the men behind him. "What th' hell? Then who . . . ?"

"Who's the man who told you all to shoot at me?" she finished his question.

"Yeah, who's he? He said he's a businessman that you robbed in Houston and took all his money and then set out after him 'cause he's carryin' some vallables you want to git off him. Who *is* he?"

"What'd he look like?" she asked.

The Texan pointed toward the station shack. "Wall, he wuz rat *thar* a minute ago. Little fellow. Kind of fat-like.

173

Had on a fancy suit that wuz white oncet upon a time."

"He's the Baron Otto vom und zum Heligendorf."

"He's the *what?*"

"He's a dangerous murderer," said Jessica. "Last night, trying to kill me and my friends, he had a man dynamite a saloon and kill everybody in it."

"Wull, shit!"

"You'd be better off helping me than him."

"Yeah. If you're Starbuck, we sure would. My name's Higgins—Lemuel Higgins. I'm glad us fellers don't shoot so good, Miss Starbuck. You know, we don't hardly ever have no reason to fire off pistols. Tried to shoot a rattlesnake here about three months ago and missed him, too."

"The baron is a dangerous man, Mr. Higgins. Did he have any dynamite with him?"

"He's got a hoss. Don't know what he might have in his saddlebags."

"Well . . ."

Higgins turned toward the men on the platform. "Don't nobuddy shoot no more," he yelled. "This here's Miss Starbuck, the girl that runs the Starbuck ranch out in west Texas. You all heard of her. That son of a bitch that told us to shoot at her's a Kraut."

Henri and Susan came up to walk with Jessie and Higgins to the station platform. Susan had managed to pull her Winchester from its scabbard as she jumped from her horse, but otherwise their horses had run away with everything they had.

"Where'd he go?" Higgins demanded of the other men.

One of them pointed. "In there. In the Peacock Palace." He was pointing at a two-story gray clapboard building— one of Alexandra's two small saloons.

"Did the train come through?" Jessie asked.

"Did it ever!" marveled a boy. "Sixty miles a hour. Never stopped."

Jessie sighed. "Well," she said, "the baron has to be rooted out of there. He is a vicious killer, responsible for countless murders."

"A'right," said Higgins glumly. "We'll he'p."

She shook her head. "It's not your fight, Mr. Higgins. It's mine. Anyway, as you showed me a minute ago, you boys don't shoot too straight. I wouldn't want any of you killed."

"We ... wouldn't want *you* killed, Miss Starbuck."

"Well, thank you. Susan, give me the Winchester. I want you to stay here with these men. Henri—"

"Don't order *me* to stand back. I won't do it," said Henri.

"All right. But, Susan, I don't want you to get hurt."

"It's my decision to make, Jessie," said Susan firmly. "Not yours. I'll help if I can."

"Well, don't take any unnecessary chances," Jessie cautioned her.

The village retreated. Jessie had sent a warning around that the baron's favorite weapon seemed to be dynamite bombs. She wasn't sure he had any, but if he did, he would surely use them. Drinkers vacated the saloons, the people left the store, families left the two houses. In a matter of minutes the town was left to Jessie and Henri and Susan, and to the baron.

The saloonkeeper from the Peacock Palace said the baron had gone upstairs. He had rented a room there earlier, and that was where he was now. The saloonkeeper pointed out the window of the room he had rented to the heavyset German in the stained white suit, and they and the saloonkeeper trotted between the two houses and out of the likely line of fire.

Jessie ran to the back of one of the abandoned houses, in through the back door, and through the house to a front window. She knelt and peered up at the window of the Peacock Palace. Henri had followed her and knelt there too. Susan was on the street, against the wall of the store, where the baron could not see her.

"He has to make a move," Jessie said to Henri. "He's trapped. There's no way out of this town except by railroad or horse. His horse is tied to the hitch rail at the station, and the train has gone up the track. He can't sneak out of town by going through the back door of that saloon. Even if he got past the people out there, you can't go out in this country on foot. He has to fight."

The baron obviously knew that too. Almost as Jessie spoke, a dynamite bomb arced from the window above the saloon and fell in the middle of the street. It exploded, throwing up an eruption of earth and dust, and the concussion broke nearly every glass window in Alexandra.

"That's just a warning," said Jessie. "Let me give him one."

She raised the Winchester and fired a shot through the window from which the dynamite had come.

Henri sat down on the floor and sighed. "We can wait," he said. "We can just leave him there. Texas Rangers will come sooner or later, won't they?"

"He'll blow up this town," said Jessie. "He'll destroy everything these people have."

"Well, they are not risking *their* lives to save it. Why should we?"

"Because we brought this trouble here," said Jessie. "Anyway, we can't just sit here. I have to know what's happened to Ki. Here, take the Winchester. Put a shot through his window now and then. Don't let him feel safe."

She left the house through the back door, trotted along the backs of the houses and the other saloon, all the way to the railroad tracks. She crossed the tracks and crawled past the platform and station, keeping herself so low she was hidden by the roadbed. When she was beyond the baron's line of vision from any window of the Peacock Palace, she trotted up the dusty street to where Susan stood pressed to the wall of the store.

The girl was grimy with dust from the explosion, and she was frightened. "Where is Henri?" she asked, trying to suppress a quaver in her voice.

"In that house," said Jessie, pointing. "You stay here. Or, better still, cross the tracks and put a little distance between yourself and the next bomb he throws."

Susan shook her head. "I'm not a coward," she said.

"No one said you were, but I can't argue with you now."

Jessie edged along the front of the store and then inside.

176

She went through, found a back door, and was just going out the back when the little wooden building shook from the force of another explosion. She ran back through to the front and outside, where she found Susan fallen and bloody, struck by flying rocks and gravel. She dragged her inside the store.

"I'm . . . all right," Susan croaked.

Startled by the squeak of a floorboard in the rear of the store, Jessie drew her Colt and rolled away from Susan, to the cover of a flour barrel. As she took aim on the door, a woman came in, glanced at her and her pistol with an expression of contempt, and knelt over Susan.

"I'll take care of this poor child," she said to Jessie. "I'll get her out of here before he blows the place up—and I suggest you do the same."

The woman was a lean, hard, sunbaked apparition in a simple cotton dress.

"I'm the minister's wife, if you're wondering," she said.

"Thank you," said Jessie.

Jessie returned to the rear door of the store building. As she had expected, the Peacock Palace had a rear door too. Which was exactly where the baron would expect her to enter. She slipped along the narrow strip between the two clapboard buildings and edged her way toward the wide-open front door of the saloon. On her hands and knees, she crawled toward that door.

Henri saw her and fired two quick shots through the swinging doors of the saloon. She could hear shattering glass inside. She put her head into the door for a quick look, then crawled in.

The barroom was, of course, deserted. Henri's two shots had broken a few bottles, and the whiskey dripped from the shelves to the floor—the only sound in the silence of the saloon. She rose to her feet and hurried across the room to the bar, where she dropped down and concealed herself from the view of the baron if he should come down the stairs.

She heard the boom of a shotgun. Someone in Alexandra had decided to join the fight, at least to the extent of firing a heavy charge of buckshot into the upstairs here.

The stairs were her problem. If she mounted them, she would be vulnerable to a shot from above, or to a bomb thrown down. She wondered if there wasn't some way to bring the baron down those stairs. She wondered if he had the least suspicion she was down here.

From where she knelt, she could see under the rude bar. There was a mess there—empty wooden cases in which whiskey had been shipped here on the railroad, a pile of dirty rags, the remnants of clothes that were the bartender's bar rags, a large box of the sawdust the bartender used to fill the boxes that served for spittoons, lots of empty bottles.

She pulled out one of the wooden cases. Working quickly, she stuffed dirty bar rags in it. Over the rags she threw handfuls of sawdust. She stood and pulled a kerosene lamp down from the shelf behind the bar. She sprinkled a little kerosene over the rags and sawdust, then shoved the case to the end of the bar at the bottom of the stairs. She struck a match and threw it in.

The box of rags and sawdust blazed fiercely for a moment. then settled into a hot, smoky fire. She threw a few more rags on top of it, and finally she poured beer over some rags to wet them, and she threw them on top. Half stifled by the beer-wet rags, the fire sent up a thick cloud of pungent smoke, which rose through the stairwell and spread into the second floor of the building.

Jessie crawled from behind the bar, quietly overturned a table near the door, and crouched behind it, where she had fresh air from the open door and a view of the stairway.

The smoke spread across the ceiling and almost obscured her view of the stairs. Still, most of it rose to the second floor.

She heard him first. He clumped heavy-footed over the floor upstairs. Then she saw him, first his feet as he made his cautious way down the stairs, then his body, and finally his face. His porcine features were twisted in rage. He held some sort of torch in his left hand and a dynamite bomb in his right. He had almost reached the bottom step before he discovered that the saloon was not afire but that the source of the smoke was only burning rags in a box. He knew it was some kind of trap, and he began to back up the stairs, searching the room with his small, angry eyes.

"Stop where you are, Baron!" Jessie yelled.

She rolled the overturned table aside and let him see her, her Colt aimed squarely at him.

"You!" he growled. "So! After all . . ."

He touched the fuse of his bomb to the flame of the torch, and a bright jet of fizzing fire spat from the fuse.

Jessie fired. She hit him, but he drew back his arm to throw the dynamite. She fired again. He fell, and the bomb fell with him, and he landed on top of it. She leaped through the door. The bomb exploded, and she was thrown to her face in the dusty street.

The Rangers came, and railroad police, and a telegram was brought by a special one-car train from Beaumont, saying the governor was on his way to Alexandra.

"We can't wait," Jessie told the people gathered around her the next day in the barroom of the Golden Eagle, the town's other saloon. "Ki and I have been away from our ranch and all our responsibilities too long. We have a long ride ahead of us."

"You are a brave and generous woman, Miss Starbuck," said the saloonkeeper from the Peacock Palace. "None of us will ever forget you."

She had given the saloonkeeper an order, payable through any Wells Fargo bank, for the money to repair the considerable damage to his saloon. She had given another to the minister of the church, to disburse to pay for all the broken glass—any balance remaining to be kept by him for his church.

She had given Susan money to pay her way to Ohio, where her widowed mother had presumably returned. Henri had suggested Susan should return to New Orleans with him, where he said he would buy her some suitable clothes for her journey to Ohio. In fact, he said, maybe he would take the responsibility for delivering her to her mother and explaining where she had been. They would go on the train.

Susan was wearing bandages on her cuts, but she limped toward the station with some vigor, anxious to be aboard the train and on her way. The railroad had said it would provide a special car at Beaumont, in which Monsieur Derval and Miss McPherson could travel to New Orleans in comfort. If it could not show Miss Starbuck that courtesy, at least it could do so for her friends.

The townsmen had rounded up the horses Jessie had bought in Galveston, and in the afternoon she and Ki mounted. They had bedrolls and other gear from the store, and Jessie looked forward to a quiet ride across the vast, open land she loved.

When the town was out of sight behind them, and their attention was given exclusively to the open land ahead, she and Ki agreed they felt relieved.

"Would you have liked to bring Susan home to the ranch?" Jessie asked.

"Would you have liked to bring Henri?" he asked in reply, holding his eyes straight ahead.

Jessie laughed.

"She will be *Madame* Derval before she sees her mother," said Ki.

"I hope you taught her well, Ki."

"I am sure he will be pleased, Jessie."

Here they are again!

LONGARM AND THE LONE STAR BOUNTY

Jessie, Ki and Longarm join forces for the third time!
Don't miss this action-packed novel featuring all three
of your favorite western heroes

coming in February!

Also, look for

LONE STAR ON THE OWLHOOT TRAIL

nineteenth novel in the exciting LONE STAR
series from Jove

coming in March!

LONGARM

Explore the exciting Old West with one of the men who made it wild!

LONGARM

Explore the exciting Old West with one of the men who made it wild!

6